$\mathcal{W}$hat time is the movie?" Morgan asked.

"I ended up talking to your father. How about if we just go down there and improvise?" Cy asked.

"Sounds great," Morgan said happily. But now that he'd mentioned Philip, she saw a window of opportunity. "Cy, what exactly does my father do?"

He explained to her about the recent acquisition by a U.S. company of Aruba's oil refinery at the southern end of the island. He said Philip's assignment here had something to do with that.

Morgan tried to figure how the five passports she'd seen in Philip's desk could have anything to do with an oil refinery.

Something was definitely going on.

JAN COFFEY

Tropical Kiss

AVON BOOKS
An Imprint of HarperCollins *Publishers*

For information address HarperCollins Children's
Books, a division of HarperCollins Publishers,
10 East 53rd Street,
New York, NY 10022.

Library of Congress Catalog Card Number:
2004095709
ISBN 0-06-076003-6
First Avon edition, 2005
AVON TRADEMARK REG. U.S. PAT. OFF. AND
IN OTHER COUNTRIES, MARCA REGISTRADA,
HECHO EN U.S.A.

Visit us on the World Wide Web!
www.harperteen.com
09 10 11 12 13 OPM 10 9 8 7 6 5

To our Taft '05 Daughters—

Kendall Adams, Michelle Bennett,
Mía Borders, Laurae Caruth, Avery Clark,
Sha-Kayla Crockett, Phoebe Dembs,
Tracy Dishongh, Madeleine Dubus,
Kelly Franklin, Amanda Frew,
Ashley Gambone, Jess Giannetto, Alex Kelly,
Arden Klemmer, Carolyn Luppens,
Meaghan Martin, Elisabeth McMorris,
Elspeth Michaels, Hana Nagao, Leah Nestico,
Monica Raymunt, Sara Rubin, Jade Scott,
Tamara Sinclair, Kate Terenzi, Lois Tien,
and Mercer Wu

May the road rise to meet you.
May the wind be always at your back.
May the sun shine warm upon your face.
And until we meet again,
May God hold you in the hollow of his hand.

Be sure to come "home" to visit!

Acknowledgments

Thanks go to Mathilde Clement, Queen of the Radisson, and Germaine Wever, Princess of all Concierges, for making our research trip to Aruba feel so much like a vacation. We are eternally indebted to you for your warmth and hospitality and for your tremendous help in finding so many fun things to do in Aruba.

Also, this book would not be what it is without the historical, cultural, or geographical knowledge of Claudio Mata, the greatest and most enthusiastic tour guide anywhere. Thanks for showing us the beauty of an island that is truly blessed and for sharing with us the friendly philosophy of Aruba's wonderful people.

Aruba rocks!

Tropical Kiss

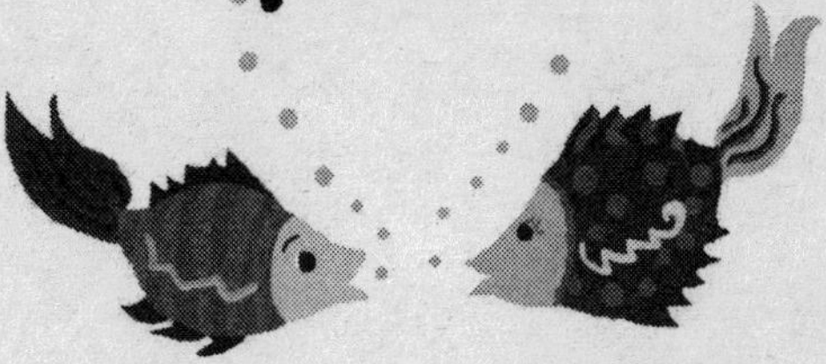

Chapter 1

June, Aruba

He was late.

The heat was giving Morgan Callahan a headache. She looked at the long afternoon rays of Caribbean sun sliding toward her along the sidewalk. The bench she was sitting on occupied one of the few areas of shade remaining on the stretch of white concrete outside the airport terminal. Sun was poison on her freckled Boston Irish skin. She avoided it like the plague.

How much longer could he be? she thought, looking at her watch.

God, it was hot.

Morgan glanced over her shoulder at the sliding glass doors leading from the air-conditioned baggage claim area. When she'd stepped out of the plane an hour ago, it seemed like the entire population of Aruba was packed into that area. Now she knew why. The air was crisp. The white floors were shining. Even the green plants in the raised dividers looked happy and healthy. And cool.

But she hadn't stayed inside. Hobbling on her crutches and pulling her bags behind her, she had come out ahead of most of the tourists.

She knew now she'd expected too much. Wished for the impossible. She'd thought Philip might just be there to pick her up. Waiting for her.

Fat chance.

Aruba's airport was not exactly as busy as Boston's Logan. The flight Morgan had come in on had been the only one arriving at that hour. There were no lines for immigration, no multiple conveyer belts running to process people's luggage. Everything came through quickly and without a hitch, it seemed. In and out within fifteen minutes. She'd stood in line longer to get a Happy Meal. A stamp on the passport and everyone was off to hotels and time-shares and whatever.

Morgan looked past the empty taxi stand at the rental car buildings across the way. The sun was blinding on the whitewashed concrete buildings. The entire place seemed deserted.

She breathed in the smells of baked Caribbean cement and jet exhaust. Gross.

Beyond the entrance to the airport, every-where she looked, the heat was giving the island that hazy, miragy look. She could see in the distance, rising sharply above the flat sur-rounding area, one high rounded hill with a little white building on top.

"Come on, Philip," she muttered, tapping her good foot on the pavement.

The sweat was trickling down the inside of the cast on her leg, and the itching was about to drive her crazy. Thank God she'd at least been smart enough to wear a light sundress. She lifted the limp blanket of hair off her neck. It didn't help. There was no breeze to cool her skin. She tied her hair back in a ponytail.

She thought of the magazine article she'd read on the plane from Boston. *The trade winds keep the island cool with year-round breezes.* Yeah, right.

Morgan leaned over and tried to get a finger down inside her cast. Why was it that the itch was always just a little farther down than she could reach? She pulled off her sun-glasses and used one of the handles. She still couldn't get at it. The sun had finally reached her, and the rays were crawling up her legs.

She gave up, gritted her teeth, and pulled her shades back on.

Behind her the sliding doors opened and she glanced around at them. A short, middle-aged guy came out. Straw Indiana Jones hat, khakis, a large untucked Hawaiian shirt. Morgan remembered seeing him on the plane. He'd been wearing his hat even then. Later on, as everyone was going up the ramp toward the Aruban customs area, he was walking a couple of steps ahead of her. He had a nose that looked like it had been chewed on by something, and the tan, leathery skin of someone who worked in construction or who had spent lots of hours in the sun, anyway. He also didn't look like he was too hot on shaving. His chin could have easily been mistaken for the butt of some aging porcupine.

Looking at him now, Morgan had no idea about his nationality. She knew he wasn't American, though; she'd noticed that he had a different color passport when he was heading to customs ahead of her.

As the doors closed behind him, he pulled out a pack of cigarettes and lit one. He was carrying only a briefcase. She glanced at her two suitcases, the backpack, and her purse. Mistake. She didn't know what the heck she'd been thinking, packing so much stuff.

Like she was ever going to leave the house during the couple of months that she was stuck here in Aruba.

She got a whiff of his cigarette smoke and immediately became annoyed. The last thing she needed was to have her asthma flare up. There was no air here as it was. Wheezing wouldn't be fun. He saw her looking at him. He smiled and started walking toward her.

Great, she thought. *American girl abducted from deserted Aruba airport.*

"*Bon tardi,*" he said.

"I don't speak . . . uh, Dutch?" she guessed, not really knowing what language he'd just spoken.

"Papiamento," he corrected. "The native tongue of Aruba."

"You're Aruban?"

"From the islands."

That wasn't much of an answer. There were lots of islands in the Caribbean.

He puffed on his cigarette and pushed back the rim of his hat.

"American?"

Wasn't it tattooed on her forehead?

"Yeah," she said, glad that she'd spread out her backpack and luggage on the bench. There was no room for him to sit down next to her.

"Your first time in Aruba?"

Morgan wished she could lie. The way he was looking at her was creeping her out. His eyes were kind of squinty, like he was sizing up some ripe cantaloupe.

"First time," she said, looking off toward the road. Two cars turned in from the main highway, but neither came toward the terminal doors.

"Boyfriend picking you up?"

"Not a boyfriend." She kicked herself after saying it. She didn't have to explain.

"Traveling by yourself?"

"No," she said right away. "Visiting family. Visiting my father. He lives on the island."

"Works for the oil company?"

"No."

He took another drag from the cigarette and blew the smoke in her direction. "Hotel business. Casino supervisor."

"No." She pulled the crutches closer to her.

They were the only two people out there on the sidewalk. She looked over her shoulder at the sliding glass doors of the airport building. The sun's reflection on them prevented her from seeing inside. She had no clue if anyone was even in there.

"Construction."

"No," she answered under her breath. He'd moved to where the bright yellow sun was behind him. She could no longer see his face because of the shadow. She decided to turn the tables on him. "Is someone picking *you* up?"

"How about if I give you a ride?"

"No. Thank you," she said tersely, guessing that he wasn't going to be much for answering questions. Still, she thought, a good defense was the best offense . . . or the other way around. Whatever. "Do you have a car?"

He held one hand out, palm up . . . like he was checking for rain. "What kind of man would I be if I had no car?"

"Then why don't you go get in your car and get out of here?"

"You can come with me."

"No," she said louder and more pointedly. "My father is coming to get me."

She could tell he was grinning at her. He dropped his cigarette on the clean sidewalk and crushed it out.

"No oil business, no hotels or casinos, no construction. I say you lie about your father. I think your boyfriend is standing you up. You come with me. I'll show you real island life."

For the first time, fear clutched at her gut. She was in a foreign country. The airport had turned into a ghost town. She had no cell phone. Great.

Not that there was anyone she could call here anyway, considering the fact that Philip had apparently forgotten she was coming to visit. Morgan looked over her shoulder at the doors again. The heck with her luggage. Maybe she could get inside. There had to be somebody. . . .

"They locked the doors when I came out," he said, following the direction of her glance. "They want nobody going in that way."

Porcupine Butt picked up her backpack and dropped it on the sidewalk, making room for himself.

He sat, she stood. It was like a seesaw. She grabbed her crutches and tucked them under her arms. She wasn't familiar with the airport, didn't know where the other entrances were, but there was no reason for him to sense her fear.

"Unda bo ta bai?"

"English, please."

"Where are you going?" He patted the seat next to him. "Sit down. Visit with me."

"I don't think so." She hobbled backward a step. "I like to be left alone. Please go."

"Pretty girl like you shouldn't be left alone."

Morgan's temper started to push past her fear.

"I don't know what your problem is, but I told you I'm waiting for my father . . . and he happens to be a high-ranking official for the United States government. He's here in Aruba on assignment, and he has important friends in high places. Very high places." Morgan wasn't going to say it, but, from what she could tell, Philip Callahan had spent his entire, boring, low-level, bureaucratic life behind a desk, pushing paper for those important people. "He should be here any minute. So unless you're looking for trouble, you'd better just leave me alone and be on your way."

The sound of a car speeding into the airport from the road jerked Morgan's head around. Immediately, her stomach sank. A new black Jaguar with tinted windows was racing toward them. She backed another step away from the curb as the car came up and screeched to a stop. She could hear Sean Paul blasting, even with the windows closed.

Somehow, Morgan doubted that Philip was in that car.

"You wait for your father. I wait for my nephew." Old Porcupine Butt was smiling as he got to his feet.

The driver revved the engine of the Jag. Even this close, Morgan couldn't see how many people were inside.

"Come with us?"

She shook her head and continued to back away. Her mind was racing. There could be two of them in the Jag, maybe three. They could force her into the car with them. She was liking this less and less. The music suddenly stopped.

As the car door started to open, she felt someone put a hand on her shoulder. Gasping, she whirled around and swung one of her crutches hard. The wood connected solidly with the knee of the man behind her. She heard him curse out loud and stagger backward.

Right away, Morgan had a strong suspicion that she might have aimed wrong. The young man holding his knee was dressed in khakis, a white polo shirt, and loafers with no socks. All in all, he looked too preppy to be very threatening, in spite of the continuing stream of muttered curses. She saw him bend over and snatch his sunglasses from the sidewalk where they'd fallen. When he looked at her, there was murder in his eyes.

"What was that for?"

"You grabbed me. It was self-defense."

"Self-defense?" he said, scowling. "I touched you on the shoulder. You weren't watching where you were going. You were backing right into me."

"You materialized out of thin air."

"I came out the side," he replied. "These doors were locked."

He was tall and had a nice build. Actually, Morgan was pretty impressed with herself for being able to knock him back a step. His brown hair was longish and straight. Handsome, but definitely too serious. At least, right now he looked pretty serious.

Morgan figured his ego had taken a bigger hit than his knees. He was still flexing his knee, but other than that he didn't seem to be in too much pain.

"It's not nice to sneak up on people," she said under her breath.

"I wasn't sneaking up on you. You backed into me." His green eyes disappeared behind the sunglasses. "You're not even going to apologize?"

"I'm sorry," she told him. "But it wasn't like I hit you intentionally."

Morgan jumped at the sound of the car door slamming. As she turned, the Jag took off in the direction of the main road. Thankfully, her annoying friend was nowhere to be seen. She'd had enough excitement. She'd just wait inside the terminal.

She hobbled back to the bench, grabbed her purse, picked up the backpack, and slung the two items onto her shoulder. The strap of the purse caught on one of the crutches. She tried to unhook it, but the backpack slipped off her shoulder, knocking over the two suitcases like a pair of dominoes. As she reached down to straighten them up, her sunglasses fell off the bridge of her nose. She tried to catch them, but the purse—still tangled up with the crutch—stopped her. Morgan pulled the purse off her arm and took a step back, glaring at the items in front of her.

"Behave," she muttered at the tangled mess of items at her feet.

"You *must* be Morgan Callahan."

Chapter 2

$\mathcal{M}$organ stared at him. He was reaching around her for one of the suitcases and obviously reading the name tag on it. She grabbed the handle, and he didn't try to wrestle her for it.

"Do you know I've been looking for you for almost an hour?" he said.

"Who *are* you?" Morgan let go of the suitcase and picked up her purse and backpack, hitching them higher on her shoulder.

"Cyrus Reed. You can call me Cy," he replied, reaching for her two suitcases. He didn't bother rolling them. Instead, in true macho fashion, he picked them up by the handles and started off down the sidewalk.

"Excuse me," she called out.

"I'm parked in the side lot," he said over his shoulder. "Stay here, I'll bring the car around."

"*Hello!*" she shouted louder. "Listen, you're welcome to my lacy underwear. But is your name supposed to mean something to me?"

He stopped and slowly turned around. "Cy Reed? Philip Callahan's assistant? Ring any bells?"

"No."

"I'm your father's assistant. A summer intern. I was told that you'd be waiting in the luggage area for me to pick you up."

"I wasn't told anything." Morgan had to be careful. The week before leaving Boston, her computer had fried and, of course, Philip's preferred way of communicating happened to be e-mail. With all that Morgan's mother, Jean, had on her plate, though, getting a new computer wasn't a priority. "But if I was supposed to meet you, then where were you?"

"I was there in the luggage area," he said shortly.

"I was there, too," she replied, matching his tone. She picked up her sunglasses and pulled them on. "And so were a couple hundred other passengers. What happened to the good old days of holding up a sign?"

"Small airport. I didn't think it would be too difficult finding you."

"Really? Even though we've never met.

And how would you know what I looked like?"

"There are a couple of pictures of you on your father's desk."

Morgan could only imagine the pictures Cy was talking about. Junior high school graduation, or maybe even earlier. It had been three full years since Philip had bothered to come for a visit. It had been about that long since Morgan had sent him any pictures, too, but she wasn't about to wash her family's dirty laundry in public. They talked—once a month on the phone for just about an entire minute. And, of course, he e-mailed her.

Morgan looked over the top of her sunglasses at him. "Do you have any kind of ID? Anything that tells me you're who you say you are?"

He shot her an irritated look, but put down her luggage and reached for the wallet in his back pocket. Morgan stared at the driver's license he stuck under her nose. "You live in Connecticut?"

"I'm a college student in D.C." He snapped the wallet closed and stuffed it back in his pocket. "I had to be somewhere else half an hour ago. If you can't make it to the lot, I'll bring the car around."

"Grouch," she said under her breath, watching him move down the sidewalk with her luggage.

It had been six weeks since her leg had gone into the cast, and Morgan was ready for the Special Olympics when it came to moving along on crutches. She wasn't going to be left behind. She definitely wasn't going to wait at some curb so that Mr. Personality could do her a favor.

The car was actually an open Jeep. Morgan reached it just as he was loading the second piece of luggage onto the backseat. He didn't seem surprised when she got there. Or, if he was, he did a good job of hiding it.

Climbing into the front seat took a little bit of maneuvering. She had to find room for her crutches and then there was a step she had to climb. To Morgan's surprise, Cy was right there, holding her elbow and helping her up.

It was easy to deal with rudeness. She was kind of flustered, though, by his help. And by the feel of his hand on her skin. And she also couldn't help but notice—despite the heat—

how good he smelled. Kind of like spice and leather.

"You didn't tell your father about that."

He was standing next to her open door, staring down at the knee-high cast. Or maybe he was checking out her legs, Morgan thought, realizing the hem of her dress had ridden up. She pulled the fabric down.

"I was planning to be out of it by the time I got down here. But my doctor didn't agree."

Actually, Morgan had been relieved. She wasn't healed. She could tell that for herself.

"How much longer have you got?"

"Two weeks."

She didn't miss the face he made before going around and getting behind the wheel. It was like he was deciding if he could live with the two weeks or not.

No more confrontations, Morgan told herself. He was giving her a ride, and she wasn't going to read anything into his looks or anything he said. As far as she knew, this was the very last time she'd see him while she was stuck in Aruba. It was only for two months or so.

She lifted her face into the wind as soon as he started driving. The sun was sinking quickly toward the shimmering surface of the western sea. The balmy air circulating around her actually felt good.

She tried to pay attention to where they were going. She hoped that once her cast was off, Philip would allow her to use his car. They were traveling on route 1B. She was impressed with the great condition of the road and the colorful buildings on either side of it. So many of them looked obviously new.

The traffic slowed to a crawl as they reached the capital, Oranjestad. *Oh-ryan-stahd*. She had read in the airline magazine that it was pronounced like that. As Morgan looked around her, she found the town downright charming. The yellow and pink and blue stucco buildings looked like a picture in a Caribbean travel brochure. The tree-lined streets were beautiful, and the town center was spotless. The sidewalks were filled with window shoppers of every size, age, and color. Restaurants were doing a brisk cocktail business at tables set outside under multicolored umbrellas, and looking up, Morgan could see more tables along railings and tanned, smiling faces looking back at her.

She looked to her left, across the divider in the road, at the harbor. The surface of the water looked like shimmering gold in the light of the setting sun. The marina was packed with everything from pleasure boats to sailboats to fishing boats.

"This is where you come if you want to go shopping."

Morgan found the comment a little annoying, and she frowned at him. He didn't look at her, though, as the traffic crept forward a little. She had reason to be annoyed, she decided. He didn't know her. He didn't know what her interests were. He was stereotyping her—she was a girl, so, of course, she could only be interested in shopping.

"Really?" she said wryly. "Do you do a lot of shopping?"

"Me? No, I'd rather have bamboo shoots stuck under my nails." He paused and shot a look at her. "You're kidding me, aren't you?"

She smiled sweetly at him and looked out at the brightly lit sign of a club they were passing. Mambo Jambo. That looked interesting.

"Is there anything else to do in Oranjestad?"

"There are a couple of museums."

"How about nightlife?"

"We just passed the theater. They tell me it has all first-run movies."

"What about the clubs?"

He sent her a sidelong glance as the traffic stopped again. "Aren't you a little young for clubs?"

Morgan bit back her answer as the driver of a silver Mercedes coming in the opposite direction planted her hand on the horn and slowed down. The windows of the luxury car opened and three blonde heads appeared.

"CY!" The driver waved madly, her hand on the horn again.

"I love you, Cy," one of them sang out from the backseat.

Traffic on that side stopped, and the passenger door of the Mercedes opened and yet another blonde in shorts and a bikini top jumped out and ran around the car. Morgan thought the blonde was about to jump the divider, but Cy gunned the Jeep, driving around the right side of the car in front of them. Hanging on, Morgan almost screamed as he drove with two wheels on the sidewalk for some twenty yards before turning down a narrow street on their right and speeding away.

"Fan club?" she asked, forcing her fingers to release their grip on the seat.

He didn't answer, and Morgan realized that he actually looked a little embarrassed.

"You don't have to answer," she said double-checking her seatbelt. "I *would* prefer to arrive in one piece, though. No more broken bones, please."

With a glance in the rearview mirror, he slowed down. After making two or three more turns, they were back on route 1B and heading north out of Oranjestad.

Morgan adjusted her sunglasses and looked at him again. With the wind ruffling his hair, Cyrus Reed looked even more handsome than she'd originally thought. She figured those girls couldn't have been much older than she was. And he was twenty. Her eagle eyes had picked that up when she'd looked at his driver's license back at the airport. Never in her life, though, would she act like them. Not even with someone she knew, liked, and was going out with.

She looked vacantly out at the passing

scenery, thinking about her ex-boyfriend. That had been Jack's complaint before he'd broken up with her the day before the junior prom. She was too stuck-up. Too cold. She wouldn't show affection in public, and she wasn't too good at it in private, either, he told her. Well, that's who she was. She definitely wasn't much of an exhibitionist. She felt safer taking her time, getting to know the person. She knew from personal experience that a heart was as fragile as a leg. She already had a cast on one. She could do without a cast on the other.

"How far are we from Philip's house?"

"Ten minutes, tops," he said. "He lives in a section called Bakval. It's a stone's throw away from the high-rise area. That's where the big hotels are. Nice beaches, too."

She smoothed a nonexistent wrinkle from her dress.

They were going around a rotary. To her left, she saw some construction going on in the distance. He pointed to one of larger buildings closer to the road. "That's the new hospital."

Morgan tucked that information away, since she knew she had to come back here in a couple of weeks to get her cast off. "How's the taxi situation on the island?"

"Very decent. The rates are set by the Aruban government, so there's no gouging."

"Cool," she murmured.

They were quickly approaching some tall buildings on their left. She figured they were getting close.

"So how long has it been since you saw your father?" he asked.

"Three years."

The sun dropped below the surface of the sea, and Cy tore off his glasses. He put them in the space between them. She had to admit, grudgingly, that he had the longest set of eyelashes she'd ever seen. They perfectly set off his green eyes. His eyes looked like jade against his tanned skin.

Get a grip, Morgan, she told herself, unhappy about where her mind was going.

"He's a very busy man, you know."

Morgan looked out at the scenery on her side of the road. The landscape was more wild here. There were fewer buildings, but she could see things looked more populated up ahead.

She told herself she didn't need to hear any

excuses, especially from a stranger who didn't know anything about who she was and how their family operated.

"I think he's going to be a little surprised."

She turned her attention back to him. "By what?"

"By you," he said simply.

Her pulse beat double-time for a few seconds. Morgan didn't know if he was trying to be conversational or if he'd been sizing her up. Was he making a general comment or paying her a compliment? She decided not to ask. There was no point. They were going their different ways as soon as he dropped her off. There was probably a gaggle of blondes in his near future.

"This place . . . where Philip lives . . . ?" Her voice trailed off.

"Bakval," Cy repeated the name.

"What kind of a house is it?" she asked.

"It's a house."

Morgan gave him a narrow look. "What I'd like to know is whether it's in a neighborhood or is it secluded?"

"It's definitely in a neighborhood."

She guessed that was a plus. They were

driving by some high-rise hotels to their left. She could see the names. Radisson. Hilton. Marriott. They had to be almost there. Morgan decided to ask the question that was on the tip of her tongue.

"Philip . . ." she started. "Does he . . . does he live alone?"

He shot her a curious look.

Morgan decided on honesty. "Look, I'm supposed to stay here for most of the summer. My mother remarried a week ago. She and her husband have extended their honeymoon to last the whole summer, and they're spending it in some little one-horse village in India."

"So, you want to know if you're going to be a fifth wheel in your father's social life?"

"I won't be a fifth, sixth, or twentieth wheel in his life." Morgan was immediately sorry for blurting that out. She forced herself to speak more calmly. "What I wanted to know is whether there's a live-in girlfriend. Is there anyone else that I should know about before we get there?"

"You didn't ask him that before coming?"

"If you must know, communication is not high on the list of Callahan qualities."

He nodded. "You don't seem to have any problem getting your points across to me."

"Are you going to tell me?"

"No live-in girlfriend," he answered.

"No roommate?"

He shook his head. "Your father does let out a small guesthouse. It's across an enclosed garden courtyard area."

"That isn't bad," she admitted quietly.

"Something's wrong with the electricity to the kitchen in the guesthouse, though. So for the past couple of weeks, they've had to share the kitchen in the main house."

"That *could* be bad," she reconsidered in a hushed tone.

"Nice guy renting it, though."

"Do you know him?"

He nodded.

"Young? Old?'

"Young."

"That could be good *and* bad," Morgan decided.

"Do you always talk to yourself?"

"Do you ever watch the road?" she asked, seeing that he was staring at her.

He shook his head in disbelief, but she

didn't miss the smile pulling at his lips. This guy got more handsome all the time. Unfortunately. Never mind her pulse doing double-time, now there was that weird fluttery action in the base of her stomach.

Cy turned right onto a tree-lined road. Behind low walls, small houses lay nestled in shaded yards. From the occasional realty signs along the road, it looked to Morgan like a neighborhood made up of a mix of islanders and vacationers. Cy made another turn onto a similar road, and a couple of hundred feet down, pulled the Jeep off the pavement onto a dirt patch between the road and a stucco wall.

"Here we go."

Morgan stayed in her seat for a minute, staring at the low, rambling villa. Beyond a wall topped with a fence, palm trees surrounding the house were visible. Lush, flowering shrubs were mixed into the landscaping. A gate led into the courtyard, and Morgan could see the top of what she assumed was the guesthouse to the right. There were no other cars near the house.

She hadn't expected Philip be there, anyway.

She looked back at what she could see of the main house. The shutters on the windows facing the road were closed. She glanced over at the guesthouse again and stepped out. The Jeep was higher than she remembered. Her left foot didn't catch up with the right one fast enough, and Morgan ended up falling on all fours in the dirt. There was nothing like a graceful landing.

"Are you okay?" Cy asked, rushing around to her.

"Fine." She scrambled to her feet, dusting off her hands on the dress. "I meant to do that."

He stood an arm's length away, not looking entirely convinced.

"Do you know the name of the person who's staying there?" she asked, motioning toward the guesthouse.

"Yeah. As a matter of fact, I do." Cy turned away and reached into the Jeep for her suitcases. "His name is Cyrus Reed."

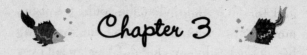

Chapter 3

Philip Callahan pulled up in front of the house at 10:15. He parked next to Cy's Jeep and turned off the engine. The lights in the main section of the villa were off.

She must be already asleep, he thought. He frowned and shook his head.

He hadn't wanted Morgan's arrival to go this way. He'd learned about the meeting he had to attend with the Aruban Governor's Office only yesterday. That was why he'd e-mailed Morgan that Cy would pick her up at the airport.

Still, Philip had hoped to get back to the house earlier than this. He'd planned to take her out for dinner. Maybe a little celebration after not seeing her for so long. Some kind of welcoming gesture. So much for that idea.

The problem was that his job ruled his life. It always had. It was the nature of the beast. His chosen profession dictated not only his daily schedule but where in the world he lived and for how long and when it was time to move again. Not too good for a steady family life. Definitely not too good for raising a daughter.

We make our choices in life, and then we live with them.

But that didn't make it any easier.

Philip was still frowning as he grabbed his briefcase and climbed out of the car. When the meeting was still going at 7:30, he knew that there would be no celebrating tonight. He'd called Morgan to tell her. Four miles or four thousand miles, the distance didn't matter. He heard the same old chill in her voice, the frosty disapproving tone that sounded so similar to that of his ex-wife. Morgan had flatly refused his suggestion to order takeout and have it delivered. Whatever Philip had in the fridge would be good enough, she'd told him coolly.

Unfortunately, he didn't remember what, if anything, he had in there. He hardly ever had a meal at home. A housekeeper came through once a week. She was usually good at checking the shelves and stocking them once in a while. So maybe there was something Morgan could eat. He hoped.

He made his way around the car and was heading for the gate leading into the courtyard when he saw the flame of a citronella torch flickering beyond the bushes. As he opened the gate, a chair scraped on the brick, and Philip saw the young man's face appear over the fence separating the two sections of courtyard.

"Long meeting," Cy remarked.

"How did it go this afternoon?"

"We missed each other in the luggage area, so she had to wait around a little bit. But I managed to find her."

Morgan had said nothing about this to him when they'd talked on the phone. He looked at the main house and then back at Cy.

"You have a couple of minutes?" Philip asked.

"Sure."

Philip cast another glance toward the darkened windows of the villa before opening the gate into the smaller courtyard. Cy was dressed in a pair of baggy cargo shorts and a T-shirt. There was a book facedown on a metal table near his chair.

"There isn't enough light out here to read."

Cy shrugged. "The air-conditioning gets to me after a while."

He grabbed a cushion off the porch and put it on one of metal chairs for Philip.

"So what's up?" the younger man asked.

Philip put his briefcase down on the chair. It wasn't easy to ask, and he had to search around for the right words. Finally, he gave up and just asked straight out. "What's she like?"

Cy stared at him for a second. "She's seventeen."

"I know that."

"She's probably changed a lot since you saw her last."

"I figured that, too."

"She has a broken leg."

Philip loosened his tie. "Really? She didn't tell me that."

"She said the cast should come off in a couple of weeks."

Already a complication. His schedule over the next few weeks wasn't exactly flexible. Damn it.

Right after Christmas, his ex-wife, Jean, had called to tell him she was getting married that spring. She'd let him know in her usual pointed way that this was Philip's "opportunity" to ask Morgan to come and stay with him for the summer. But she had also mentioned that their daughter had her driver's license and was quite independent. Living in Aruba, she'd said, Philip had never been in a more enticing place for a teenager. Morgan would probably even get a job once she got down there. He and Morgan could each do their own thing, and he could still "pretend to be a father."

Jean had never lost her way with words.

"Which leg is in the cast?"

"The right leg."

"How mobile is she?"

"She can't drive, if that's what you mean," Cy said, apparently reading his mind.

"Is she on crutches?"

"Yeah," Cy said, sitting down. "And she definitely doesn't seem to be looking for any sympathy or special favors because of it."

"How did she break it?"

"I didn't ask. I figured there might be a couple of things that you'd want to ask her yourself."

It was definitely a zing, but Philip let it

pass. He'd known the twenty-year-old since he was a kid. Cy's father and Philip had started their careers together and had stayed friends. Six years ago, John Reed decided he'd had enough of the life and returned to the States. After a stint in state government, he'd thrown his hat into a hotly contested political race. He was a first-term United States senator now. Philip knew that Cy understood the problems that went along with being raised by one parent. Although his own parents had never divorced, Cy hadn't seen much of his father while he was growing up. It was understandable that he'd take Morgan's side.

Philip pulled off his tie and stuffed it into his jacket pocket. "I have a meeting in Caracas tomorrow at noon. I'm flying out around nine."

"Does Morgan know that?"

"Not yet," Philip said. He paused. "I need to ask you to do me a favor. I want you to take tomorrow off. Spend the day with my daughter. Show her the island. Do touristy stuff."

"I don't think she's flown all this way to hang with me."

"I'm taking Saturday *and* Sunday off, so I'll

be here for her to hang out with. Tomorrow I can't, though."

"Tomorrow's Friday. I'm almost done with the spreadsheets you asked me to put together. You said you wanted the reports ready by the end of the week. That's tomorrow."

"They can wait until next week." He picked up his briefcase. "How about it?"

Philip stood waiting until the younger man gave him a nod.

"Thanks," he said, turning away.

He could feel the kid's eyes on his back as he went out the gate. He crossed the larger courtyard to the sliding glass doors leading into the open living area of the villa.

Philip trusted Cy. He knew the young man saw a lot of his own father in him, so Cy still had some vestiges of respect and desire to please. But there was also some latent distrust, even hostility, there. And there were definitely unspoken hints of criticism.

With good reason, Philip thought. But he could live with that.

Morgan had locked the sliding glass doors, but Philip had his keys. The kitchen and dining areas were all part of the same open arrangement. Two bedrooms with their own bathrooms and an office completed the layout. She had turned off all the lights, and he stood in the darkness for a moment before turning on the lights nearest to the door.

Philip looked around the room. Everything was very neat. He walked to the office and unlocked the door. Inside, he opened his briefcase and put some papers into the safe under the desk. Locking it up, he took off his jacket and rolled up his sleeves as he made his way to the kitchen.

He looked again at the open living area. He didn't know what he was expecting, but the place looked exactly the same as he'd left it. The kitchen was the same. No dirty dishes. The counters were spotless. No pairs of shoes kicked off carelessly into a corner of the red-tiled floor. No books or magazines left on the coffee table. Not a single pillow out of place on the furniture. If he didn't know better, he would have thought that no one had even been here tonight.

Philip was surprised to feel a huge knot forming in his stomach as he walked toward Morgan's bedroom. He turned on the hallway light outside the door and knocked once, softly.

He waited a couple of seconds. Hearing no response, he knocked again.

"Yes?" He could hear the sleepiness in her voice.

"Hi, Morgan. Can I come in?" There was a long pause. Philip didn't realize that he was holding his breath until she finally said okay.

He opened the door, and the light from the hallway poured in. The first thing he saw was the white cast on the leg. She had left it sticking out from under the sheets and propped up on a pillow. She sat up, and Philip saw her turn her face toward him.

Immediately, he switched on the overhead light.

"Please turn it off," she protested, turning her face.

He did as she asked, but quickly moved into the room.

"Are you okay?" Even in the half-light from the hall, he could see her eyes were puffy from crying. Her nose was red. The trash can next to the bed was filled with used tissues. He grabbed a chair by the desk and dragged it next to her.

She plucked out another tissue as he sat down.

"What's wrong, Morgan?"

She shook her head. "Nothing. I'm just too tired."

He knew she was seventeen, but Philip found himself thrown back in time. What he saw was the little girl with huge blue eyes and the freckled nose. The little girl who always cried when he came home after a long trip. She used to accuse him of not loving her. But those were the days when he knew how to win her affection back. She had never cared for gifts. She just wanted time with him. He'd given her all the time he had.

Morgan's teenage years had changed that, though. Jean's growing resentment of their situation, justified or not, had poisoned the air. Her influence had made Morgan bitter. His last visit coincided with her middle-school graduation. That had been their worst time together, ever. During the two weeks that he'd stuck around Boston, Morgan showed him that she no longer had time for *him*. She no longer cared if he stayed around or left. He was on the outside from then on. There weren't any tears. Only attitude. And the attitude was understandable.

You make your choices.

Philip focused on his daughter as she lay her head back on the pillow and pulled up the sheets, tucking them around her.

"I'm here," she said.

"I'm glad you're here."

"Yeah." She stared straight ahead. "You should go. It's pretty late."

She was right. He should go. But he wasn't ready.

"I mean it. It's good to see you."

"Thanks."

He paused. "Listen, I have to go on a business trip tomorrow. But I have the weekend booked solely for the two of us to spend time together."

She gave a small nod. "Whatever."

"Cy is going to hang around here tomorrow. He'll take you to anywhere you want to go."

"I don't need a babysitter," she said flatly.

"I know, but I don't want you to feel stuck inside here." He motioned toward her cast. "I would have left you the car, but I hear you're going to be out of commission for a couple more weeks."

"Please tell him he doesn't have to hang around. I mean it," she stressed.

"He's been working pretty hard since arriving here. He could use a day off."

"But I don't want to put anybody out."

Philip held her hand. "You're my daughter, Morgan. And I don't care how long it's been since we've had any time together. This is your house. You're not a guest. You won't put anyone out."

It was difficult to see her expression in the dark. But she didn't say anything, and Philip took it that they had an understanding.

He caressed her hair once and pushed to his feet. "Will you be up early enough to have breakfast with me before I leave in the morning?"

Her answer was slow in coming. "What time are you leaving?"

"I have to leave the house at eight."

"Maybe," she said, turning her head on the pillow and closing her eyes.

Philip left the room, actually feeling a small sense of hope. Maybe they had a chance. Perhaps without Jean around, the two of them could duel it out and get used to each other again. That would only be the first step. He had to make the most of this time. Philip Callahan's only regret in life had to do with his relationship with Morgan.

Or rather, his failure to have one.

Morgan waited until the door of the room closed before she let the tears slide down her face again. She couldn't stop them. She didn't know how to control her emotions. It always had been like this. She guessed it would be like this forever.

By the time she was in the third grade, she no longer cried when he went away. As she got older, she realized that she'd made herself believe that she didn't care that he had to go. She had her mom. She knew now that not caring was just her way of dealing with it. But seeing him again—and the anticipation of seeing him—still crushed her. It made her remember how much she loved him, how much she felt she deserved to have her father be part of her life. But when he came, it hurt her because she also always knew how short their time together would be. When he came home, it was just a matter of time before he went away again.

Morgan blew her nose and shut her eyes, forcing the tears to stop. Her ex-boyfriend Jack had called her "cold." He said she had no emotions. If he'd ever seen her like this, he'd have thought differently.

She took a deep breath and wiped away a last escaping tear. So far, this had been a monumental disaster of a year. More times than she could count, the rug had been pulled out from under her.

First, it had been Jean's announcement about her marriage. Then, the plans for their honeymoon and where Morgan was going to spend the summer. If all of that wasn't bad enough, Jean had informed Morgan that they'd be moving in with Kabir in the fall. She'd have to change high schools for her senior year.

For the first time in her life, Morgan truly felt like a fifth wheel in her mother's life.

Things had just gotten worse after that. Jack had broken up with her the day before the prom. Then, the next day, Morgan had tripped over her own dress and fell down the

stairs at her mother's townhouse. She'd
ended up with a broken leg.

A total disaster, but also a blessing. It gave
Morgan a good reason to cry about everything that had gone wrong with her life.

The cast on her leg was supposed to help to
heal the bones. Morgan knew she had to try to
do the same thing with her heart, but there
was no plaster made that could protect that.

Sure, she was here with Philip, she told herself, but things would be different now. She
was older. She didn't need him. Still, he was
her father, and he'd said he was glad she was
here. Maybe he meant it.

Maybe she would give him a few days. See
if he really did mean it.

If he didn't, it would be easy enough to
close the door again. But this time, she'd slam
it shut and throw away the key.

Chapter 4

It was twenty minutes to seven when Cy heard Philip Callahan's car drive off.

He lay back in bed, listening to the staccato whistle of an oriole singing outside his window. The small black-and-yellow bird was pretty, and could really sing out. Even Pavarotti wouldn't sound this good at 6:40 in the morning.

Philip must have gotten an emergency phone call to leave so early. It sure as heck didn't take two hours and twenty minutes to get to the airport. He did seem to get a lot of those phone calls that sent him flying out of the office. Especially for an accountant.

Cy liked Callahan. He was a pretty decent guy. It was a good opportunity, too, to intern for an official in the U.S. Department of Energy. Callahan's specific duties centered around the import of oil. The way Cy understood it, he was a kind of specialist. One-of-a-kind expertise, Cy had been told. As a result, Callahan moved around a lot. Aruba's oil refinery, on the southern end of the island, had been purchased recently by a U.S. company. Callahan's assignment here had something to do with that.

So far, that was as much as Cy knew about what the older man did. Of course, he'd only been on the job for three weeks. If his own tasks were any indication, though, there was a lot of number-crunching and paper-pushing involved.

At around 8:30, Cy padded barefoot across the courtyard to the villa. The sliding door was open. He could see all the windows had been opened, too. The air-conditioning unit was silent.

"We'll see how long that lasts," he murmured. The air was pleasant now, but this looked to be another day with no breeze. Cy knew that in another hour or two, the heat and humidity would be brutal.

He called a loud greeting into the house, but as he poked his head inside, he could hear the shower running in one of the bathrooms. He stood in the doorway for a minute, considering whether he should leave and come back in a little while. He didn't want to scare Morgan.

As he turned to go, the phone started ringing. He knew Philip's answering machine would pick up, and after three rings, it did kick in. But it disconnected and the phone started ringing again a couple of seconds later.

The shower continued to run. After the third time of the rings starting and stopping again, Cy figured someone was probably trying to get hold of Morgan. As far as he knew, it might have been Philip.

He walked in and picked up the phone as it started ringing a fourth time.

"Hello. Callahan residence."

"Thank God," a woman's voice said over the wire.

The connection was horrible. It sounded like she was talking into a tin can. A big tin can, from the sound of the echo. It had to be an overseas call.

"Philip, is that you?"

"No. Mr. Callahan is not home right now. Would you like to leave a message?"

"No. No." There was a pause. "Is Morgan Callahan there?"

"Yes, she is, but—"

"Would you be kind enough to put her on the phone?"

"She's in the shower. Would you like me to have her call you back?"

"No, that would be very difficult. I really need to speak with her now."

"Oh, wait a minute." He listened again. The shower had stopped. "I think she's done. Hold on, please. I'll see if I can get her for you."

"Morgan," he called loudly, approaching the bedroom with the phone in his hand. "You have a phone call."

Her bedroom door was closed, so he knocked. "Morgan."

Cy thought he heard her voice. It sounded like it was coming from the bottom of a deep well.

"What?" he called.

She said whatever it was again, but he couldn't make out the words.

The bedroom door was unlocked. He poked his head in. The bed was made. The suitcases were open on the desk and on a luggage stand.

The closet doors were left partially open, and it looked as if she was half unpacked.

"Morgan?"

"I'm in the bathroom. I need help."

He wasn't sure he heard her right, but he crossed the bedroom.

"Did you say you need help?"

"Yes." She sounded frustrated. "My foot is stuck. Please help me."

The woman on the phone was saying something, giving him some kind of instructions. Cy dropped the phone on the bed and approached the bathroom door. He tested the knob. It was locked.

"You have to unlock it," he said through the door.

"I can't. I told you, my foot is . . . my cast is wedged between the bathtub and the toilet."

"How did you do *that*?"

"When I stepped out of the tub, I slipped and . . . It doesn't *matter* how I did it. It just happened. And I'm stuck. And I'm starting to panic. And that's not a good thing. I have asthma, and even though I haven't had an attack for a while, stress is one of my triggers. And right now, I'm feeling really stressed.

And it's *really* hot in here. And I—"

"Morgan," Cy said sharply. "Stop talking. I'm going to get you out in a couple of seconds. It's no big deal."

He reached above the door frame, searching for the small pin-shaped key that used to be above every door in his family's house while he was growing up. When Cy was a kid, his younger brother's middle name had been mischief, and the monkey liked to lock himself up. So, as a family, they were always prepared.

This was Aruba, though, not Connecticut. There was nothing on the ledge. He looked at the doorknob again. It looked the same as the ones at home.

"You can't get me out. Can you?" she asked. There was definitely a touch of panic in her voice.

"Of course I can." Maybe something thin and sharp would work. Cy wondered if Philip had a toolbox.

"You're lying. I'm stuck here."

"I don't lie."

"I can hear it in your voice."

"You don't know me well enough to read that kind of stuff in my voice." Cy said. "Just hang in there. I'll be right back."

"You're not going to leave me here, are you?" she said, her pitch rising.

"I'm just going to the kitchen for a second."

"Great," she said. "While you're having your breakfast, be sure to make yourself some coffee and . . ."

While she was still talking, he hurried to the kitchen and opened cabinets and drawers in search of anything that might do the job. Morgan called his name couple of times.

"I'm coming," he shouted back, grabbing a very thin meat skewer.

"I don't have an inhaler with me," she was saying as he reentered the room. "My chest is getting tight."

"Morgan," he said calmly through the door. "I'm getting you out. Now, talk to me. Tell me something."

"What?"

"Anything," he said, sticking the tip of the skewer into the hole. It fit in the small hole. Good so far.

"My mind is blank." She paused for a second. "And no wisecracks from you."

"I wouldn't think of it." Cy moved the piece

of metal around in the lock, trying to feel for the little button that he needed to push to unlock it. "Tell me about your high school."

"No."

"Why not?"

"It's not my high school anymore. I have to go to a different school for my senior year."

"How come?"

"My mother is moving into her new husband's house when they get back from their honeymoon. I have to live with them."

Just as he almost had it, the metal rod slipped out of his hand and fell with a clatter to the floor. He picked it up and pushed it in again.

"Tell me about your friends."

"I don't have any."

"You're lying."

"I don't lie."

"Then tell the truth." He crouched down to get a better grip on the skewer.

"I don't have any."

"Why?"

"Well, because my mother wouldn't trust me enough to let me stay with any of them for the summer. And since I'm going away to a new high school next year, why would they want to have anything to do with me anyway?"

"Because they're your friends." Cy heard the click and stood up.

"You don't know much about . . ."

He opened the door to the sight of her naked back. She screamed, and he scrambled to shut the door.

"What do you think you're doing? You can't come in. I don't have anything on."

"You didn't tell me that before," he said in self-defense.

"I was taking a shower. What did you expect?"

"Don't you have a towel in there with you?"

"Of course I do, but I can't reach it. My foot is stuck, remember?"

He stuffed his hands into the pockets of his shorts and shook his head, smiling. "You're a piece of work."

"What did you say?"

"I said, tell me exactly what you want me to do."

"That's not what you said," she replied in a reprimanding tone.

"Would you like me to go?"

"No," she said quickly. "I'm really stuck here. And I don't want to break anything again."

"Instructions, Morgan," he asked.

"Well, you have to throw me a towel."

"Where is it?"

"There's one hanging from the bar on the wall behind the door. It's just out of my reach."

"Most people put a towel within reach before getting in the shower." Cy smiled again as he heard her mimicking his words back at him under her breath. "How am I supposed to throw you a towel?"

"Close your eyes. Reach around the door and hand it to me."

"You trust me to do that?" he asked, amused.

"What . . . to keep your eyes closed? You'd better. Besides, there isn't much here to see. Trust me."

He *had* seen, and she was wrong. But he wasn't going to correct her on that count right now.

"Okay, here we go." He opened the door, closed his eyes, and put one foot in.

"Close your eyes."

"My eyes *are* closed." He stepped into the bathroom, his hands out in front of him. "I thought there wasn't much to see."

"Just keep them closed. Turn to the right."

One hand by mistake brushed against her skin. She was wet. And she smelled great. She pushed his hand away.

"Hey! I meant my right. Your left. The towel is behind the door."

Cy tried to not think of what part of her body he'd just touched. He turned to the left. Reaching out, he touched the towel and pulled it off the wall. As he turned and took a step, though, his foot caught on something and he felt his other foot slip out from under him. The next thing he knew, he heard his head crack on the wet tile and he was lying flat on his back.

He had a hazy image of long red hair brushing over him as the towel was wrenched out of his hand.

"Are you okay? You should be more careful."

"Careful?" he asked, lifting his head to see what he'd tripped over. "What are your crutches doing in the bathroom?"

"I need them to get around."

He lay his head back on the tile floor. He

could feel a lump already growing on the back of his head. He looked up at her. Morgan had the towel wrapped tightly around her, and she was sitting on the edge of the toilet. She had long, beautiful arms and shoulders. His eyes traveled up her neck to her mouth.

"You don't look too good," she said, reaching down to touch his forehead. "You aren't going to pass out on me, are you?"

He caught her hand. It was a strange feeling. All of a sudden, he needed to touch her. She looked too beautiful to him to be real.

"Cyrus," she said more sharply. "Snap out of it, will you? I can't even get to a phone to call 911. I don't even know if they have 911 in Aruba. Please!"

"The phone!" he said, letting go of her. "Somebody is on the phone for you."

"They'll have to wait. I'm still stuck." She reached down and helped him as he sat up.

He felt the back of his head, stretched his neck, and turned around to see how she had gotten herself so jammed into that little space. The culprit seemed to be the bulky plastic bag she had wrapped around the cast. It was also caught on a plumbing valve behind the bowl.

He started to pull it away.

Her hand touched his hair, and she felt the lump on his head. He winced.

"I'm sorry."

He shrugged, not wanting to look up. He was at a total disadvantage, sitting there. He didn't particularly mind the feel of her fingers in his hair, but the rest of her was too much of a temptation.

"I promise to not make a habit of this."

"Of what?" he asked. The plastic cover came free. He figured she could probably pull her foot out now, if she tried. But he didn't tell her that.

"Of hurting you."

He looked up into her face and smiled. "You think you're a tough guy?"

"Very tough. So, maybe it'd be safer if you keep your distance." She bent over her knees to check his progress. The smell of soap and scented shampoo went right to his head. Their faces were inches apart.

"I think that'll be a little difficult."

Her gaze met his. "Why is that?"

Her eyes were the indefinable color of the waters of the Caribbean on a clear day.

"You're the boss's daughter. And his instructions to me were to stick close to you."

"I don't particularly like that."

"You don't want me hanging out with you?"

"I don't want you to do it because it's Philip's orders," she responded, sitting up straight again. "I don't need a keeper."

"I'm afraid you do." He touched her cast. "At least, until this thing comes off."

"Wrong again. You *and* Philip," she said seriously. "I've been living with this thing for six weeks. I only missed one day of school because of it. I've been doing it all. Climbing stairs, getting on the subway, catching the bus."

"Taking a shower."

"Accidents happen. I was new to the place. It won't happen again." Morgan moved her foot and realized she was free. "You've done a wonderfully heroic act. Now, don't you have to go to work or something?"

"No, I have the day off." Cy pushed to his feet and stretched a hand out to help her. She shook her head and stood up on her own.

"Then you should go off and visit your friends. Do whatever you do on your days off."

Cy hadn't realized until that moment how crowded they were in the bathroom and how small the towel was that she had wrapped around her. She was a knockout. "I'd just as soon hang around *you* today, if that's okay."

She followed the direction of his gaze, and a blush began to rise from the top of her chest onto the skin of her neck and face.

"That may not be such a good idea." Morgan pushed him out of the bathroom ahead of her. "Now, out of here. Out of my bedroom."

He stopped when he saw the phone on the bed. "I don't know if they're still holding."

"It doesn't matter. If it was important enough, they'll call back."

Hopping behind him, Morgan ushered him out of the bedroom. Outside in the hall, Cy heard the click of the bedroom door lock and smiled.

This would be too much fun to miss. He was definitely sticking around today.

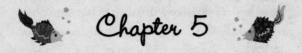

Chapter 5

Every inch of Morgan's body was tingling, and she couldn't understand why. It wasn't like her to feel this way. Of course, no one had ever looked at her like that before, either. Not even Jack.

She dropped the towel onto a chair and grabbed a pale yellow sundress from one of the open suitcases. Pulling it over her head, she carefully sat on the bed and reached for the phone.

"Hello."

"What's his name?" her mother asked.

She gasped, even muttered a curse. "What are you doing spying on me like this on your honeymoon?"

"About five minutes ago, I was starting to get a little nervous about the cost of this phone call. But every time I decided to hang up, the conversation between you two kept getting better and better. So what's his name? How old is he? And what in heaven's name is he doing in that house? You two aren't alone, are you?"

"How was your flight over, Jean? How's Kabir?"

"He's fine. But you're changing the subject. And that's *Mom* to you."

"Can I talk to him?" Morgan asked.

"No. At least not right now. I want some quick answers, young woman."

Morgan tried to think of what her mother might have heard. What might have been considered inappropriate. There wasn't much.

"He's a college student in D.C. doing a summer internship with Philip. He rents a guesthouse next door . . . actually on the same property. He's twenty. I only arrived yesterday. There isn't really much more that I know about him."

"Athletic?"

"Yes."

"Tall?"

"Yes."

"Handsome?"

"You're getting way too personal, Jean," Morgan asserted.

"Fine. Don't tell me. What's his name?"

"Cy Reed."

"The Reeds of Darien, Connecticut?" Jean asked. "It has to be."

Morgan tried to remember the address she'd seen on the driver's license. "I think so. Do you know them?"

"Of course I know them. I know Cy. You know him, too."

"I don't think so. I'm getting old, but not senile. I've never met this guy in my life."

"You definitely have. You've been to their house."

Morgan sat up straight on the bed. "You're getting ahead of me. Start all over again. How do you know the Reed family?"

"Cy's father and your father have known each other for a long time. They were best friends. John Reed was the best man at our wedding."

"Now that's a bad omen, if ever I heard one."

"Don't say that. They're a very nice family. I've lost touch with them since the divorce. What are the parents up to? Where did you say Cy goes to school?"

"Why don't I put him on the phone, so you can talk to him instead?"

"Are you being sarcastic?"

"No. Not at all," Morgan said, trying to keep her tone natural. She *was* being sarcastic. And she *was* still disappointed with her mother for not trusting her enough to stay in Boston. "How's India?"

"We haven't left the airport yet."

Morgan tucked the phone between her ear and shoulder and found some underwear before hanging more of her clothes. Her mother went on to tell her every detail of the flight, including what she ate and read on the plane.

It was like a reality show, except nothing happened.

As Jean talked, it occurred to Morgan that she never once asked how Morgan liked Aruba. Her mother didn't seem to want to know how she and Philip were getting along after three years of separation. Even if Jean asked, though, Morgan didn't think it was worth mentioning that she had yet to spend *any* time with her father. Despite his invitation for breakfast, he was gone when she'd woken up this morning. She'd found his short note on the kitchen counter. Something about an emergency at work.

An itch down inside her cast was driving her crazy. She grabbed a metal hanger she'd straightened the night before and pushed it down along her skin. As always, the itch was farther than she could reach.

"This phone call is going to cost you more than if you'd flown me to India," Morgan said finally, encouraging her mother to hang up.

"You're right," Jean responded, sounding pouty. "But I don't know when I'll be able to call again. Kabir says the phone system in some of the areas we'll be visiting can be a little shaky."

"Aren't you visiting his family? You gave me a number there."

"We are, but we'll be taking some side trips for sightseeing, too."

"Sounds great."

After a few more minutes of advice and warnings, Jean finally hung up.

Afterward, Morgan walked around the room, busying herself with putting away more of her clothes and wondering if Cy might still be around. Another five minutes and her curiosity won out.

He was in the kitchen, sitting on one of the

high breakfast stools and reading the paper. Morgan didn't miss the two bowls of cereal and glasses of juice on the counter.

"Expecting company?"

"Yeah . . . you."

His gaze wandered down over her dress, and Morgan had to stop herself from looking to see if she'd left a button undone or if there was some tear somewhere. He looked back at his paper. He had a way of flustering her.

"I might have had breakfast already."

"You might have, but you didn't."

He motioned with his head toward the dishwasher. "Nothing in there."

Morgan had skipped dinner last night, and this morning—finding her father gone—she'd been too angry to eat. She was starving now. She let the crutches rest against the wall and made her way to the counter.

He closed the newspaper and went to the fridge, getting the milk. "Sorry there's not much of a selection. Your father doesn't usually eat breakfast, and I'm happy with a bowl of cereal."

"This is great." She watched him as he poured the milk. As she looked at him she tried to find a resemblance to pictures she'd seen of his father. Her parents' wedding photos had been some of her favorite things to look at while growing up. She remembered seeing John Reed in them.

"Do I have something sticking out of my ear?"

She shook her head and turned her attention to the bowl of cereal. "Did you know we've met before?"

"Of course."

"You did?" she asked in shock.

He ate a spoonful of cereal and nodded.

"Why didn't you say something about it before?"

"When was I going to mention it? We only saw each other yesterday afternoon, and this morning just didn't seem to be the right moment."

"You could have said something yesterday. It certainly would have made me feel a little more comfortable."

"I don't think so." He shook his head. "My clearest memory is you skinny-dipping in my parents' pool with me."

She sputtered and nearly choked.

He slapped her on the back. "Don't you hate when the milk comes out your nose?"

"No way," she got out between coughs. "You're making that up."

"You hadn't brought your bathing suit with you, but we decided to go swimming anyway. I was a gentleman, though, and kept my trunks on."

"I don't remember any of this." Morgan managed to say, catching her breath. She looked at him suspiciously. "How old was I?"

"Two . . . maybe three. I was six. I remember it like it was yesterday."

"Adolescent." She poked him with her spoon.

He was smiling, and she had to be careful. His smile was contagious and lit up the room like a hundred-watt bulb. She could feel the heat.

"That was your mother on the phone?"

She nodded.

"Is she enjoying her honeymoon?"

Morgan nodded again.

"You're okay with everything?"

She shrugged. "It's not my life. It's Jean's. Kabir is good for her."

He just listened, waiting for her to say more.

"Kabir Shuklah Shah. He's from India originally. He teaches engineering at MIT. A very nice man. Quiet, brilliant really, and happy to let his wife control and manage their life. They're perfect for each other."

"And where do you fit in?"

"I don't really know yet. I definitely didn't fit in this summer."

"That's why you're here?"

"The two of them are honeymooning in India . . . sightseeing and visiting with some of his family." Morgan took a sip of her juice. "This fall, we'll just see what happens. I told you that I'm supposed to change high schools and move in with them."

"And you're not happy about it."

"I don't know how I could be." Morgan put her spoon down, realizing that she didn't feel like she had to mince words with him. "The reason I'm upset, though, has nothing to do with my mother's marriage or whether I like or don't like Kabir. I'm not even all that wound up about changing schools for my senior year."

She pushed the food away.

"What I'm ticked at is her lack of trust . . .

her inability to show any flexibility."

"What did she do, or didn't do?"

"I didn't want to come to Aruba."

"Oh, right." He made a face like he didn't believe her.

"Philip and I are strangers. He doesn't want me here any more than I want to be."

"How do you know that?"

She stared at him for a second and then gestured to the interior of the villa. "Do you see him here?"

Cy didn't answer.

"And it wasn't like there were no other choices . . . no other places for me to stay for the summer."

It wasn't like Morgan to vent like this, but he'd asked.

"My best friend lives in Weston, twenty minutes outside of Boston. Becca's mom asked me to stay with them for the summer. And it wasn't like Jean didn't know them. Becca and I have been friends since sixth grade. But she refused. She was determined that I come here. She . . . she is so wrapped up in the idea that she's done her job, and now it's Philip's turn to be a parent."

He shook his head.

"But I'm not ten years old," she continued. "I'm seventeen. I don't need a parent, and he doesn't want to be one. I don't belong here. I don't *want* to be here. This whole situation is so wrong. "

Morgan closed her eyes for a second, then took a deep breath. She'd said too much, become way too serious. "I'm sorry. I shouldn't have unloaded all this on you. Please don't ask again. You should just know we're a very dysfunctional family."

His hand closed over hers.

"Look, Morgan. You're stuck here for the summer, but it doesn't have to be a waste. Aruba's a great place. We just have to think of a few things to do to make it bearable."

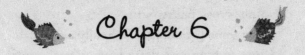

$\mathcal{M}$organ was sure she'd hate Aruba, but Cy loved it. And he was determined to change her mind.

As they talked about it, though, he began to realize how tough that might be.

She didn't like sun and wasn't crazy about sand. She couldn't go swimming until the cast came off. It was the same with all the water sports activities, too. Tubing, windsurfing, parasailing, snorkeling, scuba diving—all totally out of the question. She claimed sailing or any kind of boat rides made her seasick.

She was trying to be difficult, but Cy knew that had more to do with her parents than with this island paradise.

He wasn't giving up.

Cy had been thinking about giving her the twenty-five–cent tour of some of the popular tourist stops, followed by a big lunch. He might even possibly introduce her to some of the summer brats they would

71

certainly cross paths with.

After some prodding, she finally agreed.

"Just so long as I don't have to get out of the car if I don't want to."

"Of course."

"And only if I definitely don't have to admit to anyone that I had a good time . . . just in case someone asks me at a later date."

"That goes without saying," he said, smiling back at her.

There were dozens of American high school kids and college students whose families had houses down here. They worked or just bummed around for the summer on the island.

If he were asked, Cy would have to admit that he didn't think too highly of some of them. Like everywhere, the summer set included its share of airheads, self-focused princesses, and weed-smoking morons. But there were some fun people that he'd met here, too. Those were the ones he'd started to hang with on occasion. With any luck, they'd run into some of the good ones.

It was 10:30 when they finally got on the road.

"I was going to give you an all-day whole-island tour, but I've changed my mind," he announced as they pulled away from the villa.

"That's good—I won't last for an all-day anything," she said. "I demand to be fed at noon."

He considered skipping the tour and taking her out for a second breakfast, but then quickly decided against it. Her mood changed so quickly, he wasn't sure when he'd be able to get her in the car to see the island again.

At the end of the road, they turned south on the main highway. "Isn't this the same road we drove on last night? The one from Oranjestad?" she asked, looking around.

"Yeah, it is."

"Then how come that sign we just passed said this is route 1A? Last night it was 1B?"

"One of the peculiarities of the island. The roads that have numbers are *A* going one way and *B* going the other. I figure they must do that to make it easier for the mail delivery."

The sun was already hot, but the breeze from the open sides of the Jeep felt good. She'd tied her hair in a ponytail and was wearing a straw hat over it. She had on the same yellow sundress she'd been wearing at breakfast. Spaghetti straps and a knee-length skirt—pretty conservative compared to what the other American girls wore on the island. But she looked darned cute in it.

At a stoplight, she took a tube of sunscreen out of her bag and started applying it to her arms.

"I guess you know how to keep that skin from burning too badly."

"Yeah, I've had to live with it for a while."

His gaze followed the motion of her hand as she spread the cream on her neck, down the neckline of the dress. "Do you ever tan?"

"Not really. I burn. I get sun poisoning. I peel. Then it starts all over again."

"Maybe we could break the cycle," he said, taking the cream out of her hand and looking at the SPF. It was thirty. "This won't cut it. Let's go with sixty."

He pulled into the parking lot of a convenience store and told her to wait.

Morgan tried to not make any noise or melt into the seat as Cy spread some of the sunscreen he'd just bought on her shoulders and back. His hand was warm. His fingers not only smeared the cream, but dug gently into her muscles. It felt absolutely wonderful. She held her hair above her head as his fingers moved up and massaged it onto her neck.

"So where are we going?" she managed to get out. Her voice sounded a lot like a croak.

"I thought I'd take you to my favorite place on the island."

"Okay," she said softly, taking the tube away from him.

"Can you handle the rest of it?"

Morgan nodded reluctantly. She would have loved to have him continue with what he was doing, but she was a coward. She put dabs of cream on her arm and watched him get the Jeep back on the road.

As they drove south, Cy told her a little about the section of the island that they were leaving behind. He talked about Malmok, where the wealthiest people and most Americans connected to the resorts lived. He told her about the lighthouse at the northernmost tip of Aruba. He told her about the sand beaches and the golf course with its surrounding villas and homes.

His feeling was that the northern part of

the island wasn't really representative of what the most of Aruba was like, but she'd see that for herself.

It wasn't long before they turned left and started inland. Morgan noticed a difference in affluence right away. The houses were smaller, but they were still well-kept. As they passed little villages, Cy explained that the islanders who lived here *seemed* to have less, but everyone he talked to said they had everything they needed. Real poverty and crime were pretty much nonexistent on the island.

"And Arubans take a lot of pride in their island," he told her. "They feel like they've been blessed with so much, even though they don't really have any natural resources to speak of."

"Aruba seems so dry," she commented looking at the sparse vegetation on the hilly landscape they were approaching. "It's not lush and green like you normally picture when you think of a Caribbean island. It kind of reminds you of Arizona."

"That's true," he said. "And they consider that one of their blessings, too."

"How is that?" she asked.

"One guy who gives tours here told me that

the lack of water made it less appealing to conquering Europeans, who set up slave plantations on other islands. There were still Europeans here, though. The Spaniards used it for raising horses, then the Dutch took it, then the British, the Portuguese, and the Spaniards again. The Dutch ended up with it."

"On the plane coming over, I read an interesting article about the native heritage," Morgan told him. "Something about archaeologists finding artifacts dating back forty-five hundred years."

"Yeah. Stuff from Arawak Indians or their predecessors. And they've been coming here from South America ever since the Stone Age. As recent as the early 1900s, about one-third of the island's population was non-European. Once you're out of your cast, I can show you some rock drawings and carvings at Fontein Cave and around Cunucu Arikok. I think the whole thing is pretty cool."

Morgan considered it a good sign that Cy was planning on still talking to her two weeks from now. "So, where exactly are we going?"

"The eastern side of the island, also known as the windward coast."

"Is that a figure of speech, or is there actually a breath of wind there?"

"There is wind and plenty of it."

"But only nine months a year," she said, finishing the sentence for him.

"Wait and see."

Morgan wasn't convinced. She just wasn't sure she was built for a place like Aruba. At least, not in the summer. Her arms were sizzling from the rays of the sun. She spread more cream on them . . . and thickly.

"Our jet circled the island at least a half dozen times before landing. There didn't seem to be much of anything on the eastern shore."

"Most of it is parkland. A lot of rock and cactus and brush. The wind and the tides are actually so strong on that side that the beaches aren't the safest for swimming." He shrugged. "To me that's part of Aruba's charm, though. You have nature—wild and almost untouched—right over the hill from some of the calmest water and the most beautiful beaches in the Carribbean. "

"Beauty and the beast, huh?"

"Yeah, and now you get to meet the beast."

The Jeep reached the crest of a hill and

suddenly Morgan felt the wind change. No longer just the effect of the moving vehicle, the air was immediately cooler. The breeze whipped her hair into her face and almost blew her hat right off her head.

The sea glistened in the morning sun. The white-capped surf was heavy here, with rolling breakers crashing in explosions of foam against the shore. The sound of the sea was in her ears as well, and for the first time, she could smell salt in the fresh air. As she looked at the gorgeous sight, Morgan didn't think she'd ever seen so many shades of blue and turquoise.

Cy drove the Jeep down the winding road toward the shore. As they descended toward the base of the hill, she could see a large white building and a parking lot. It looked like it was built on the edge of a cliff of light-brown rock. The pavement looked almost white in the sunlight as well, and a small tour bus and a dozen cars were parked along a fence on one side of the lot.

"The air is actually cooler," she said.

"Wait till we get down there, then you'll really feel the difference."

"This is your favorite place in Aruba?" she

asked as Cy pulled into the lot.

"Well, one of them," he responded, pulling the car in against a low, stone wall. "Aruba is so beautiful, it's hard to have just one favorite place."

Morgan looked back at the white building. It was a restaurant and tourist shop. She looked back at him, somewhat perplexed.

"Not the shop," he said. He pointed to a rock formation beyond the wall. "They call *that* the Natural Bridge."

Morgan looked across at the flat-topped arch of rock stretching over the incoming waves. The arch had been carved out by the force of the wind and the waves, and it was truly a magnificent sight. Morgan saw a couple of younger children holding their arms out like wings against the wind as they walked across the bridge. To her right, a narrow sandy beach was being steadily pounded by the waves passing under the bridge. There was a gazebo-like building there on the beach. She looked back at the sea and was speechless for a couple of minutes, stunned by the sheer beauty and power of the spectacle.

"Does this meet your definition of wind?"

She nodded. "Let's get out."

"Of course," he replied, but Morgan was already climbing out of the Jeep. This time she was careful, though, and didn't put on another show of landing on her hands and knees. By the time Cy came around, she had the crutches tucked under her arms and was heading toward the bridge. He fell in beside her.

The wind was so strong that she took off her sunglasses and hat. Reaching the rock-strewn bridge, she moved across until she was in the middle of the span. Facing the water she closed her eyes and soaked in the feeling of the wind and the sun and the spray from the boiling sea below.

There was something very cleansing about standing there. It was as if she could give up her thoughts, her soul, all of her troubles to the power of Nature.

She understood why Cy liked this spot so much.

Finally, she looked at him. He was standing beside her. Watching her. "I don't think I've ever seen any sea or ocean so . . . so . . . impressive, I guess," she said over the sound of the wind. "It's amazing."

"This is definitely very cool. Watching the waves come rolling through the arch from down there is pretty impressive, too. But I don't think you want to do all those stairs today."

He was pointing behind them at the beach and the gazebo. A long set of wooden steps led from the parking lot to the beach. As they walked to that side of the bridge, Morgan noticed a tall blonde woman come out onto the beach and start waving madly at them.

"I think someone is trying to get your attention."

Cy looked and after a lengthy pause waved back.

The woman pointed up the stairs.

"I think she wants to meet you at the top of the stairs."

"I'll be right back," he said, a note of reluctance in his tone.

Morgan watched him make his way off the bridge. The wind mussed his hair and his khaki shorts flapped as he walked. The shirt he was wearing molded to his body, outlining the muscles. His feet were in a pair of leather sandals. Perhaps it was all this gale-force wind at the Natural Bridge, but suddenly the prospect of being stuck in Aruba for a couple of months and having a specimen as handsome as Cy Reed as a friend, neighbor, and . . . whatever . . . wasn't too bad.

Her bubble burst with the same speed that it had taken shape.

The blonde finally reached Cy at the top of the stairs. Wrapping herself around him, she put a lip-lock on him like the wife of a sailor whose ship had just come home from a *very* lengthy tour of duty.

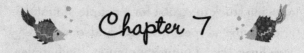

Chapter 7

Kate Leicester's assets were pretty obvious.

She had the body type of a Barbie doll. She was a natural blonde with bronze skin and deep-blue eyes. She was nineteen and going into her sophomore year at Georgetown — exactly a year behind Cy.

Unfortunately, she also seemed smart, funny, and even pleasant when she'd been introduced to Morgan — in spite of the fact that she'd caught her boyfriend bringing another woman to their favorite spot. But of course, being perfect, Kate was also forgiving.

Morgan learned more about Kate than she truly cared to know in a span of about twenty minutes. There was no avoiding it. She was stuck in the silver Mercedes with Kate's constant companions — Liz, Beth, and Ellie. She'd listened politely for what seemed like an eternity as they drove to wherever it was they were all having lunch. Kate had generously offered to change places with Morgan . . . to give her a break from the sun.

She must have gotten some sand in her cast because the itching was worse than before. Morgan tried to stick a finger down in there. She tried one arm of her sunglasses. She banged on the side of the cast, but nothing worked.

She didn't know why it was that anytime she was feeling a little down in the dumps, her leg would start to act up.

To stop herself from going insane, Morgan clenched her hands in her lap and pressed her back against the seat.

The Mercedes was comfortable and Morgan recognized it as the car that Cy had fled from yesterday on their way back from the airport. But she was quickly becoming tired of all the not-so-subtle hints about the long-standing relationship between Kate and Cy. It didn't matter. The three friends just chattered away, coming back again and again to the point they were trying to get across.

It was a done deal. Case closed. The coffin securely nailed shut. Cy Reed was off-limits.

Morgan got the point.

She was also ready to go home. She couldn't wait until they got back to a town or anywhere that she could catch a taxi back to the house.

Aruba was such a small island, her wish came true within moments. They stopped at an open-air café at a quiet intersection of a sunny little town the girls called Santa Cruz. As they piled out of the car, four other people they all knew were just getting up to leave.

Morgan tried to look interested during quick introductions in the parking lot. Two of the young men's names she didn't get. Another one was an athletic-looking guy named Nick Bloch. There was also a young woman with very short, brown, curly hair. She was introduced as Mackenzie Spencer. She had tomboyish looks and beautiful, dark olive skin. She also made a point of coming over and actually shaking Morgan's hand.

Cy disappeared to use the bathroom. A quick look around, and Morgan realized that, unlike the streets of Oranjestad, there was no steady stream of cabs going by. Seeing Mackenzie getting into a car by herself sealed her fate. She hobbled over and asked if the young woman was going anywhere near Bakval or Oranjestad . . . or wherever she could find a cab.

"I don't have to be at work until two. I'll take you wherever you want to go," she offered.

Morgan told Ellie to pass on a message to Cy about something coming up and got in the car.

"Mac," the young woman told Morgan as soon as they were on the road. "My friends call me Mac."

"Mac. Great name," Morgan commented, relieved to be leaving the lovers and their bodyguards behind. "Thanks for the ride."

"No problem," she said, looking at her carefully. "I take it you're not a great fan of the Lizards?"

Morgan looked at the other girl. "The Lizards?"

"The Lizzes."

She smiled and shook her head. "I don't get it."

"Elizabeth, Elizabeth, Elizabeth, and Elizabeth." Mac nodded back toward the restaurant. "They're all Lizzes. Liz, Beth, Ellie. All of them are named Elizabeth. So is Kate. She's Elizabeth Katherine Leicester."

"You've got to be kidding." Morgan laughed as Mac shook her head. "Do you think that's a requirement of being their friend? You have to be named Elizabeth?"

Mackenzie nodded. "That and being blonde and doing a pinkie-swear that you'll always dress and look and talk the same."

"Wow. I didn't realize what a privilege it was that they allowed me to ride with them."

Mac looked at her seriously. "That wasn't a privilege. That was a preplanned misinformation session."

"Excuse me?"

"We all knew you were coming. Cy announced it last Saturday when we got together for lunch after windsurfing."

"What did he say about me?"

"That you're his boss's daughter and that the two of you would be living at the villa for the summer."

"Oh, great!"

"Well, the Lizards wanted to make sure they nipped in the bud any ideas you might have."

"Well, it worked." Morgan stared at Mac's profile. "Kate and Cy are an item. I got the message."

"I said it was a *misinformation* session. Cy's story is 'been there, done that, turn the page, just friends.' And I believe I heard him say something about never making that mistake again."

"Really? She seems perfect."

"All I know is what Cy told me. He says he and Kate had a brief fling last fall back at Georgetown, and that's it. Over and out."

"They told me in the car that those two have been inseparable since Kate started at Georgetown. That she decided to spend the summer in Aruba instead of going to her family compound in Maine because of him. Because he asked her, they said."

Mackenzie shook her head. "I don't want to be unfair. Most of the time, the Lizards are bearable, and Kate is nice. But she seems to have some kind of hang-up about Cy. But that's her. I wouldn't totally write him off until he has a chance to explain his side of things."

Morgan shook her head. "There's no need

to explain anything. Not to me." She stared ahead. "I only arrived yesterday. There's really nothing—"

"Look," Mac said, giving her a friendly smile. "You don't have to make up your mind ahead of time about what will or won't happen this summer."

"This summer?" she stammered. "I . . . I . . ."

"It's okay. I saw the look you gave him at the restaurant." Mac steered around a rotary. "Don't worry. Your secret's safe with me. All I'm saying is just keep your options open and don't let the Lizards intimidate you."

It surprised Morgan how well they'd hit it off.

She shouldn't have been surprised. Mac-kenzie was a straight talker and seemed to have a wisdom that Morgan didn't see in too many people.

Mac worked at a sandwich and pizza shop called The Brick Oven. The open-air restaurant was on the same street where all the high-rise resort hotels were located. It was definitely walking distance to Bakval from there, but a little too far for someone in a cast, and Mac insisted on dropping Morgan off at the villa.

All was quiet at the house. Too quiet. Morgan put away the rest of her clothes and wrestled her suitcases into the closet. She wandered around looking at things. It wasn't long, though, before she decided to take Mac's offer and stop back at The Brick Oven for a late lunch.

After calling for a cab, she threw a paperback novel and a towel and sunscreen into her backpack. If it was nice there, she decided, she'd just spend the entire afternoon.

The pizza shop was charming, with tables set out on a veranda facing a green landscape of palm trees, flowers, and swimming pools of the resort hotel across the road. Morgan sat at a table under an overhead fan and felt the stress of her morning begin to melt away.

Mac introduced her to the owner of the restaurant, who, it turned out, was Mackenzie's mother, a native Aruban woman with a beautiful smile and Mac's dark eyes. The three sat and chatted for a while until Morgan took their suggestion and walked to the beach across the street.

This was the Caribbean that Morgan had always imagined. Straw umbrellas provided complete shade for those who wanted it, and the white sand beach was soft underfoot. Vacationing families and honeymooning couples and people of all ages and descriptions lounged on the comfortable chairs and splashed in the water. The boats and colorful parachutes of parasailors dotting the beautiful blue-green sea just completed the picture.

As she sat down, Morgan became a believer. Aruba was beautiful.

Between the views and the book and the feeling of complete comfort, Morgan soon lost track of time. She only realized that the afternoon was slipping by when Mackenzie got off work and joined her on the beach some time later.

Just sitting there and talking, Morgan was amazed how much the two of them had in common. They were both seventeen. Mac's father was American and, like Morgan's family, her parents were divorced. Mac rarely saw her father, especially in recent years. She'd graduated this year from the International School on the island, though, which gave Mac some additional things to think about.

"Now that I'm looking to go to college, my dad has offered to have me come and live with him. I could study in the United States."

"Where does he live?"

"California."

"Are you going to do it?"

Mac shrugged. "I don't know yet. We're kind of strangers. But it's either that or go to the university in Holland. A lot of the kids here go that route, but I'm not sure it would be right for me. I don't have any family there."

"That's important to you?"

"Family is very important to Arubans. When kids grow up and get married, they almost always live in houses very close to their parents . . . even if they work at the other end of the island."

Morgan told her about her friends in Boston and the life she had there. Mac explained what it was like living on an island year-round, and told Morgan her feelings on having seasonal friends.

As the sun started to sink toward the horizon, the throng of people on the beach began to thin out, and Mac offered to go and buy a couple of salads for dinner from a beachfront café some hundred yards away. There was a light breeze blowing now, and the music of a reggae band floated across the water from a pier just down the beach.

"Mañana . . . sí. ¡Te dije mañana!"

The sound of the man's voice made Morgan sit up in her chair. She looked over her shoulder, and the hair on her neck immediately stood up on end. The man from the airport, Old Porcupine Butt, was talking on a pay phone on the walking path that ran in front of the hotels.

Everything about the man gave her the creeps. Morgan glanced hopefully in the direction that Mac had disappeared. There was no sign of her.

Morgan sank down in the chair as the man turned in her direction. He was still talking on the phone, and she desperately hoped he hadn't seen her. At least the beach wasn't as deserted as the airport had been yesterday. Still, she could do without listening to his hustle. He was so sketchy.

Morgan put on her straw hat and pulled the rim down over her face. She tried to focus on the rhythms of the reggae band and ignore the sound of his voice.

A couple of minutes later, she felt a shadow fall over her and almost jumped out of her skin. Looking up, she was relieved to see Mac carrying a tray loaded with salads and drinks.

"Are you okay?"

Morgan glanced over her shoulder. Old Porcupine Butt was gone.

"I'm fine."

"Are you sure?"

She nodded, helping Mac put the food down. "I got myself spooked over nothing."

They listened to the music and chatted, and Morgan watched the multicolored lizards and bright-green iguanas sitting on the edges of the concrete paths enjoying the last of the sun's warmth. No one paid the least attention to the little creatures. *No more than a person would look twice at a squirrel in Boston*, Morgan thought.

An hour later, they were still sitting and enjoying the balmy air. Morgan was amazed that, despite the darkness, there were actually growing numbers of people going up and down a path that ran along the beach, the same path that she'd seen Porcupine Butt on.

"Each of the resort hotels has a number of very nice restaurants," Mackenzie explained. "And then, of course, there are the casinos."

"So there is a lot to do at night on the island?"

"Of course," Mac replied with a smile. "The national motto of Aruba is 'No worries, just parties!'"

It was 10:30 before they decided to go. As Mackenzie drove her home, she explained that every Saturday morning, if it was breezy— which was most of the time—she windsurfed with friends. She also told Morgan that Cy was a fanatic about windsurfing, too.

"You should come and watch. It's a good time."

Morgan shook her head. "Philip and I have some catching up to do over the weekend. I'll go with you another time."

As they pulled up to the villa, Morgan saw Cy's car and another parked there. For a couple of seconds, she wondered if the car belonged to Kate, and an uncomfortable feeling settled in the pit of her stomach.

After saying good-bye, she walked through

the gate into the courtyard and spotted the two people waiting for her. Both appeared to be foaming at the mouth.

Philip and Cy looked ticked.

Morgan decided to resort to the usual family practice. No explanations and no confrontations. She waved, smiled like nothing was wrong, and headed for the door of the villa.

Chapter 8

Morgan opened her eyes and tried to focus on the white phone next to her pillow. She had no idea how long it had been ringing.

She vaguely recalled thinking about calling Becca last night. She must have fallen sleep, she decided, while she was trying to remember if there was any time difference to Boston.

She reached over and answered the phone, but realized immediately that Philip had already done it. He was talking to another man in a language that she didn't understand. She wondered if it was Papiamento, the native Aruban language she'd heard Old Porcupine Butt speak at the airport. She disconnected and looked at the bedside clock. It was already 8:30.

Morgan considered going back to sleep, but then she could hear pots and pans banging in the kitchen.

"Guess it's time to face the music," she muttered, getting up.

Looking at her reflection in the bathroom

mirror, she was amazed that in spite of the gallon of sunscreen she'd slathered on yesterday, she still showed touches of color on her face and the tops of her shoulders.

But at least it was *color*, not third-degree burns, she reminded herself.

She was extra-careful coming out of the shower that morning. Try as she might, though, Morgan couldn't help dwelling a little on what had happened yesterday . . . and how angry Cy had looked last night.

She hadn't been able to escape completely after being dropped off by Mackenzie. Philip had come to her door, obviously restraining his anger. It was a good thing he did, too. Still, he'd told her that Cy had been looking for her for most of the afternoon. Since Philip had gotten back from work, the two of them had been looking together.

The message Morgan had left for him apparently hadn't been passed on with any clarity by the Lizards. Cy had been under the assumption that she'd taken a cab home. Mac hadn't even been mentioned. The rest was history.

Morgan had apologized to her father. She figured she had to do the same to Cy.

The smell of real breakfast was drifting out from the kitchen by the time Morgan came out of her bedroom. Philip appeared to be in the middle of doing three things at the same time—toasting bread, flipping pancakes, and frying bacon.

Morgan paused as the smells triggered something way back in her memory. Her mother was a cereal person, but Philip had always liked to cook breakfast for his daughter. She used to love it.

She cleared her throat. "I heard Cy say yesterday that you aren't much for eating breakfast these days."

He looked up, noticing her for the first time. "I like to save myself for special occasions."

Morgan realized that this was the first time they were seeing each other in the daylight. He looked good, fit, and handsome, much as she remembered him. A touch of gray colored his sideburns, but he still had a head full of dark wavy hair. His eyes were as blue and intense as ever. Morgan looked like her mother, except for her eyes. She had inherited Philip Callahan's baby blues.

He seemed to be doing some reminiscing,

too, as it appeared that he'd forgotten the current pancake on the grill.

"Do you need a hand with that?"

He looked at the pancake and flipped it. It wasn't too burned.

"Can you butter the toast?"

She nodded, approaching. "How many people are you cooking breakfast for?"

"Just the two of us."

Morgan was disappointed that Cy wasn't coming over for breakfast, but then she remembered what Mackenzie had said about the windsurfing.

She leaned her crutches against the fridge and started helping him. They worked in silence. Morgan realized that they'd been away from each other so long that there wasn't even small talk they could share.

Philip made the effort, though. "So, did you enjoy yourself yesterday?"

They hadn't gotten to that last night. Morgan decided to be honest. "I did. The girl I met—Cy's friend—was really nice."

"Mackenzie."

"Yeah. She drove me here, and then I met her later by the high-rise resorts. Her mother owns a pizza place over there." She named the place.

"I know The Brick Oven. I've stopped there a couple of times for takeout."

"Mac's mother said I can have a part-time job there for the summer if I want," Morgan told him. "I'm going to take her up on it."

Philip paused and looked at her for a moment. "Don't you want to wait until your leg is out of the cast?"

"No, not really. She said I can manage the cash register for now. I'll wait tables in two weeks."

"Do you still like your eggs over easy?"

Morgan nodded, relieved that he wasn't objecting to her getting a job. She took out dishes and silverware. Looked inside of the fridge for juice. There was quite a selection. "You went shopping?"

"Just bare-bones stuff. There's a pad of paper on the counter. You should write down whatever it is that you need or want. Clotilde is the housekeeper. She comes over every Monday. She takes care of the shopping, too."

Morgan noticed there was some writing

on the pad already. It was an address in San Nicolas.

She'd heard about San Nicolas. It was a town at the southern end of the island. Mackenzie had mentioned it and said that the area was where a lot of workers at the refinery lived. She'd also said there were some rough sections in the town.

"Sorry, that's mine." Philip snatched the pad off the counter and tore off the top sheet, stuffing it into his pocket.

Morgan thought he seemed a little jumpy about the note, but she shrugged it off.

As they sat at the counter for breakfast, Philip seemed preoccupied, but she decided not to hold it against him. He'd made a point of making her breakfast. She decided to return the gesture by trying to make conversation while they ate.

She told him about Boston and her high school and how she'd already started looking at some colleges. He seemed to perk up at that. He even started asking some questions about her preference as far as majors and the size and location of the schools she was thinking about.

He definitely looked impressed when Morgan told him she was thinking of pursuing her education in engineering.

"I've always been good at math and science," she said.

"I'm not surprised," he responded. "You got the genes for it from—"

He stopped as the telephone rang in another part of the house.

"Sorry, the handset is in my room," she said, quickly realizing the phone Philip had used was sitting on the counter. But that wasn't the telephone that was ringing.

Philip excused himself and headed to his office. Morgan hadn't been aware that there was a separate phone there. It was the first time that she'd seen the door of the office left open. She'd checked the door yesterday and found it locked.

She could hear snatches of conversation. This time she could hear him speaking in Spanish. Three years of the language in high school allowed her to pick up a few words here and there. Money. Next week. Meeting. Morgan looked toward the office just as Philip closed the door. That was the end of her eavesdropping.

She looked down at the plates of food he'd made. They hadn't even made a dent in them.

It was some time before he came out of the office. He didn't have to say anything. She saw it in his expression. He had to leave.

She decided there wasn't any point in getting upset. It was what she'd come to expect, and she would just put up with it.

For two months.

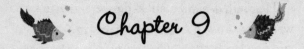

Chapter 9

Cy's foot touched something as he started to unlock the guesthouse door. It was dark outside, so he opened the door first, dropped his duffel bag inside, and turned on the porch light before looking.

It was a plate of cookies, wrapped in cellophane. A folded piece of paper was taped to the top. He reached down and picked up the plate. It was still warm. He smelled it. The cookies were homemade. He smiled and read the note.

Sorry about yesterday—Morgan

He walked across the courtyard to the villa.

A single light had been left on in the kitchen. Cy immediately saw the note that was taped to the sliding glass door.

To anyone who cares to know where I am,

It's Saturday night and Mackenzie is dragging me yelling and screaming to someplace called Carlos 'n Charlie's. She tells me my appreciation of Aruba can't start until I've experienced that atmosphere.

Hope to see you there . . . whoever you are.

He smiled at her stick-figure signature. It was a picture of a saucer-eyed girl with crutches and one leg in a cast. Cy figured the note wasn't left for Philip.

Heading back to the guesthouse, he saw another note taped to one of the outdoor lounge chairs.

Dear Neighbor,

I'm sorry. And I'm at Carlos 'n Charlie's. I'm writing this just in case you're taking a break en route from your car to the house and haven't seen my other notes.

Morgan

P.S. The cookies are homemade by me. Hope you like them. I almost set the kitchen on fire making them. BTW, the sketch is a self-portrait.

P.S.S. (or is it P.P.S.?) Two full days, and I'm still not burned. A miracle. Thank you.

Cy had planned to stay home and cool it tonight. But Morgan was doing a great job of tempting him.

From the outside, the place looked like a saloon you might see in an old Western. Morgan paused and corrected herself. In old movies, there were never lines of people waiting to get into those places. Even though there was a porch with a handful of tables and chairs, there had to be fifty people trying to get inside Carlos 'n Charlie's.

While they were heading for the line—which moved surprisingly fast, Morgan thought—a wildly painted Party Bus pulled up and a crowd of young people piled off, joining them on the sidewalk. The music was blasting out the open front door.

The way Mackenzie explained it, the club served Mexican food until sometime in the evening, and then they pushed the tables and chairs to the side and the place became one giant dance floor. And that was every night. Morgan's crutches came in handy in getting sympathy from the bouncer at the door. He waved them in ahead of other waiting customers.

"They didn't card us," she told Mac as they were pushed into a large room filled with people.

"You can get into most clubs at sixteen in Aruba." She had to yell her answer to be heard over the loud music.

Morgan looked around her in amazement. A

master of ceremonies in a flowered shirt was standing on a platform to their right, next to the bar, and singing into a mike while three guys with bottles balanced on their heads tried to do a kind of line dance behind him. He was encouraging the audience to sing along. Participation was not a problem. People on the dance floor, some of them standing on chairs, were singing at the top of their lungs with the music.

"I think it's safest if we move to a corner."

Morgan agreed and followed Mackenzie through the noisy throng of revelers. As they skirted the edge of the black-and-white checkered dance floor, her crutch landed on someone's foot. Morgan turned to apologize to the dancer, only to back into a high table, nearly toppling a woman who was dancing on it. The woman regained her balance, luckily, but not before dumping half of a margarita onto the bald head of a thirty-something tourist standing beside the table. The drenched guy started yelling, the woman started yelling back, and Morgan tucked her crutches closer to her side and scrambled after Mackenzie.

"I think you almost got caught in the middle of a brawl," Mac shouted, looking back at the dance floor as Morgan caught up to her.

"I think I started it."

Mac just grinned as if she didn't believe her. Just then, a middle-aged couple got up from a table in the corner, and Mac grabbed the table.

"Is it always this crazy?" Morgan asked, leaning her crutches against the wall.

Mac leaned over and yelled in her ear. "Actually, this is the quiet part of the night. Wait till later!"

Morgan sat on the high stool across from Mac and looked around with interest. The brawl she'd started was over. The bald guy was nowhere to be seen, but the same woman was still dancing on the table again with a fresh drink in her hand.

Morgan had never been clubbing before in a bar like this one. People continued to stream in, and she looked up at a glassed-in booth above and to one side of the door. She hadn't noticed it when they'd come in, and she watched the DJ flip through records.

There was so much to see. Every inch of the walls were covered with framed 1950s photographs of people standing next to huge fish, posters of old advertisements for Mexico and

Cuba, and funny bumper stickers. The entire place was vibrating to the music.

A shrill whistle made her jump up in her seat. Looking around, she realized whistling was how the waiters got people to move out of their way as they went between the bar and the tables and the kitchen with orders. She shook her head in amazement at Mac.

A whistling waiter made his way to their table and took their drink orders.

Neither of them ordered alcoholic drinks. Mackenzie shouted something about being the designated driver, and Morgan yelled back that she needed her wits about her to make sure she didn't end up with another broken leg. It didn't seem to make any difference to the waiter, and he went whistling off toward the bar.

While they were waiting, Morgan watched as the dancing and singing continued. A balcony ran around three sides of the place, and she could see people up there, drinking and eating and people-watching. She knew there were people above them, too, because a group of girls in the middle of the dance floor was looking up and laughing and shouting back and forth over the music with someone.

Morgan had never seen so many people having such a good time. Maybe Mac wasn't kidding when she said that Aruba loved to party.

Their drinks came, and the two of them got wrapped up in another contest that the flowered-shirted guy on the stage started.

It was a couple of sodas and another act later when she saw Mackenzie wave to someone by the door. Morgan's heart did a flip as she recognized who'd just arrived.

"You met Nick yesterday, where the Lizards stopped for lunch," Mac said excitedly over the noise. "I can't believe he's here."

Morgan looked again and realized that Cy had come with a friend. The two had spotted them and were weaving their way over. She turned to Mac to ask a question and immediately noticed her friend's nervousness.

Mackenzie ran her fingers through her curls and took a long sip of the soda. She took off the little sleeveless sweater she was wearing over her sundress and immediately put it back on. She moved her purse from the table to the back of the chair, and put it back again on the table.

"I think I'll go to the bathroom," she said.

Morgan put a hand on Mac's arm. "You're not going anywhere."

"But—"

"What's going on?" Morgan asked with a smile.

"Don't say anything," Mac warned as Cy and Nick arrived at the table.

Morgan turned around to greet them and bumped her crutches. That was all it took, and she watched helplessly as disaster unfolded. The crutch fell toward Cy. As he reached down to catch it, the crowd of dancers surged behind him, sending him forward and causing him to trip over the crutch.

Scrambling off the stool, Morgan put herself in his path to catch him. It only made things worse, though, as he fell into her and they both went down, taking a waitress who was passing with them.

One upended chair and a couple of pictures knocked off the wall. Thankfully, the waitress's tray had been empty. Morgan was the only one who actually hit the floor, landing solidly on her butt with Cy on top of her.

Immediately, Cy was up on his feet and bending over her with Mac and Nick looking on. Before pulling her up, he felt her arm and then her leg, making sure she was okay. She was more embarrassed than anything, though their little tumble wasn't spectacular enough even to attract attention beyond the closest tables. The music continued to blast and the handful of people who had first turned around went back to whatever it was they were doing before.

Before she could bend down to get her crutches, he picked them up.

"These could be considered weapons of mass destruction," he yelled to her before placing them securely in a corner.

"Twelve days and I'll be burning them."

"I want to help. I think I should be the torchbearer."

"You've got the job," she said with a smile.

Cy ushered her back onto her stool, and she was introduced again to Nick Bloch. With the noise level as it was, there wasn't much opportunity for conversation across the table. Nick left the table and came back in a minute carrying two more stools he'd stolen from somewhere. He set his close to Mackenzie's. She seemed flustered but happy.

Cy dragged his next to Morgan's. He said something that she didn't hear. He bent his head close to her ear.

"What are you drinking?"

His hair was wet. The clean scent of shampoo mingled with his spicy cologne. She didn't think she'd ever smelled anything so wonderful.

"Soda," she managed to say.

"Not a drinker?"

She shrugged. "I can try things at home, but I don't like to drink."

He didn't hear her. "What?"

Morgan put her mouth close to his ear. "I get into enough trouble without it. How about you?"

His arm looped over her shoulder, and he kept her close as his face turned to her. "I'm not a *big* drinker. No bingeing. Don't believe in it. But I'll have a beer or two."

Their faces were so close, their foreheads were practically brushing. Within moments the music, the crowds, even their friends across the table . . . none of them existed for Morgan. It was just the two of them, and she just wanted to be lost here in this moment forever.

"Thank you for the cookies."

"Sorry about yesterday," she said in answer.

"You shouldn't have run off like that."

"I know," she admitted. "I just have this thing about not wanting to be in the way."

"That fifth wheel thing."

She nodded.

"Well, you weren't. Kate and I are not—"

"You don't have to explain."

"Yeah, I do." His green eyes fixed on hers. "We went out a handful of times in D.C. last year. It didn't work out. She's been after me to try again this summer. But I'm not interested."

Morgan was thrilled but tried to keep her face calm. "She's really beautiful," she said for lack of something better to say.

"I guess. But she's . . ." He shrugged. "I don't know, she's like something you see in a jewelry store display case. It might look really good under the glass, but once it's out in the open and you get a close look, it's not quite the same."

Morgan knew how she herself would look under close scrutiny, and it wasn't too good.

Mackenzie and Nick moved. Morgan saw her friend motion toward the dance floor. The emcee in the flowered shirt was taking a break.

A slower dance song came on, and people were pairing up.

"Is Nick a good guy?" she asked Cy.

He nodded. "I only met him this year. Really good windsurfer."

"I mean 'out of the display case.'"

He smiled. "You looking after Mackenzie's interests?"

"Maybe," she replied. "I like her. She has a lot going for her. When it comes to men, though, I'm not sure she's as worldly as the Lizards."

Cy laughed out loud. "The Lizards, huh? I wonder who they might be."

Morgan explained to him what she'd been told by Mackenzie. "But back to Nick . . ."

"He's from California. Goes to school at UCLA. Engineering major. A year older than me. Has a job here for the summer, working in construction. As far as I know, no girlfriends. We both arrived on the island about the same time, three weeks ago."

"Does he like Mackenzie?"

He glanced at the dance floor and smiled. "I don't know. You tell me."

She followed the direction of his gaze. Nick

and Mackenzie were wrapped in a tight embrace. Her head was resting on his shoulder. His arms had a tight lock on her. "I'd say he may be partial to her."

Cy seemed amused by her comment. "This is a side of you I didn't see the first day."

"I'm starting to feel comfortable, so watch out. You never know what side of me comes out when."

"I can't wait." He stood up, tugging on her hand.

"Where are we going?"

"The dance floor."

"With this?" she asked, pointing at her cast.

He nodded. "I'm feeling a little partial, myself. Thought I'd show it, if you don't mind."

Nothing could have shut Morgan's mouth more effectively than his words. She stood up, and he shook his head when she tried to reach for the crutches.

"You won't need them. You've got me."

Chapter 10

It felt completely normal to get up on Sunday morning and find Philip gone again. Nothing could possibly make her feel bad this morning.

She didn't bother to take a shower, but pulled on a thin bathrobe over the T-shirt she used as a nightgown. Taking her crutches, she went to the kitchen. A note from her father — with a cell phone on top of it — sat on the counter.

I'll be back in a couple of hours, and the phone is yours, the note read.

"A couple of hours from . . . when?" she asked loudly, glancing at the clock on the wall. It was 9:10.

She picked up the cell. It was a flip phone. Much fancier than the one she used back in the States. Morgan wondered if she could take it back to Boston at the end of the summer.

As she was looking at it, a phone started ringing in the house. She quickly realized it was coming from Philip's office. After the second ring, she decided to answer it and made her way to the door. It was locked.

The ringing stopped. She tested the door again. It wouldn't budge. She hadn't really looked at it before, but the lock on this door was much different than the other locks in the house. It was a deadbolt lock that obviously needed a key. But there was also a security keypad.

"Ooooh," she murmured, "a secret chamber."

A sharp knock on the sliding glass door behind her made Morgan practically jump out of her skin. She whirled around and saw Cy standing on the veranda.

For a brief couple of seconds, she panicked about the way she was dressed. But she figured he'd already seen her standing there, so there was not much point in hiding. She went to open the door for him.

"Good morning," she said shyly.

He answered her greeting by leaning down and brushing a kiss on her cheek.

The blood rushed to her face. She quickly went toward the kitchen, hoping he wouldn't notice. Of course, she did have to stumble over one of the high chairs by the counter. She recovered, though, somewhat gracefully.

Last night had been a dream. Morgan didn't know how long they'd danced in that place. It didn't matter. She'd been floating for most of it.

Mac's curfew was midnight, though, so they'd all left together in time for her to get home. Nick had gone with Mac, and Cy had taken Morgan.

Driving back, Cy turned on the radio. They'd wrestled playfully over the choice of stations, but Morgan was preoccupied. She didn't know what would happen when they arrived at the villa. She didn't know if he would kiss her or not. She knew she wanted him to.

The decision had been taken out of their hands, though, when they found her father waiting for them in the courtyard.

"Did you sleep well?" Cy asked now.

"Too well," she said, turning and looking at him across the counter. She put her crutches next to the fridge. "We have more options for breakfast than just cereal this morning. Philip went shopping."

He was looking at her that way again. Morgan knew she hadn't left a button undone. That time was gone. She now felt soft and warm all over.

"I'm pretty good at making eggs," she offered.

"Sounds good. I'll help." He came around the counter, but then paused as his ankle came in contact with one of her crutches. "Eleven days left, buster."

He liked eggs over easy, too, so that made it simple. They divided the jobs. Cy set the plates out and made toast while Morgan cooked the eggs.

The area behind the counter was tight, and they kept bumping into each other. Every time he moved, she was aware of his presence. It was all she could do to keep from burning the eggs.

It was after one of those collisions, as they were bowing and apologizing, that Morgan saw him pause. The look was there again, that sharp-edged glint of desire in his eyes. This time she did glance down. Her robe had fallen open, and he was looking at the T-shirt she was wearing. Her underwear was just visible beneath the hem of it.

She closed the front of the robe and tightened the belt. "Sorry. I should have taken a shower and changed. I wasn't expecting—"

He kissed her. A soft kiss on the lips that teased her with the promise of more. A lot more.

"Around me, you can dress like this anytime."

Morgan restrained herself from attacking him right there. This was all new to her, actually wanting someone to touch her, kiss her. It had never been like that with her ex-boyfriend. She'd always looked for reasons *not* to be alone with him. She'd used every excuse she could think of to keep him from getting too touchy-feely. That was when he'd called her cold, incapable of showing affection.

It wasn't true. She now realized that the problem wasn't with her. Jack was just wrong for her.

"Oh, no! The eggs!" She reached for the frying pan with her bare hand and immediately realized her mistake. Cy was right behind her with a pot holder as she jerked her hand off the iron handle. He took the pan off the stove and flipped the eggs onto the toast he'd laid on the plates.

"Impressive," she said, putting her burned fingers to her mouth. "You've done this before."

"Let me see that."

"It's no big deal." She held back her hand.

"Morgan," he said in a more authoritative voice. "Let me see what you did to your hand."

"It's fine. See? Nothing." Like Pinocchio's nose, the blisters on the red skin grew as they looked at it.

"Come with me," he ordered, dragging her toward the door.

"Wait a minute. The eggs are getting cold." She planted her feet. "Seriously, I can't go out looking like this."

"Yes, you can."

"No, I can't."

She gasped when he lifted her by the waist and carried her to the sliding glass door. He opened the door with one hand and before she knew it, she was outside.

"You're being a bully." Her feet touched the ground by the table and chairs in the courtyard.

"You asked for it. Now sit."

"Seriously. It's fine."

He pulled up a chair behind her and pushed Morgan down onto the seat.

As soon as he bent over one of the large plants and broke off a leaf, she knew what he was doing. "Aloe?"

"Yup."

"You could have asked nicer. I would have walked out here by myself."

He smiled and crouched down before her. "I enjoyed it. Now give me your hand."

She put her hand on her knee and watched him split open the fat leaf he'd taken from the plant. Aruba was covered with aloe plants. She remembered reading somewhere that at the beginning of the twentieth century, Aruba was the largest producer and exporter of aloe in the world. A picture of the plant was even on their national coat of arms—or maybe it was on their flag. Anyway, it was important.

The liquid inside was clear and gooey, almost like a gel. But when he put it on, it felt cool on her skin, and the burning stopped immediately. Then she caught a whiff of it.

"This is foul."

"No, it's not."

"It's gross. Seriously, I have to wash it off." She tried to get to her feet. He put both hands on her shoulders, keeping her down.

"Don't be a baby."

"I'm not. But it smells horrible. No self-respecting person would want to get within a hundred yards of me."

"It's not horrible." To prove his point, he leaned toward her, but he didn't smell her hand. Instead, his mouth found hers.

It felt so right. Morgan's arms wrapped around his neck. She was lost in the moment, in the taste of him. Her mind emptied of everything but him.

He pulled back from the kiss. She felt kind of dazed, wanting more. He took her hands from around his neck and put them on her lap. Perplexed, she looked up into his face. He leaned over and whispered in her ear.

"I just heard your father's car pull up in front of the house."

Morgan bit her lip to hide a smile and closed the front of her robe tighter on her chest before standing up.

The whole thing was really pretty amusing. Yesterday, she was complaining that Philip stayed away too much. Today, she actually wished he would have taken his time getting home.

Not really, she thought as she walked with Cy back to the villa. She was looking forward to giving those eggs another try. For the three of them.

$\mathcal{M}$organ's schedule was ideal. She would be working the cash register from approximately 10:00 to 5:00, four days a week, and Mackenzie's mother told her she had the option of picking up more hours at night and on weekends if she wanted as the summer progressed. Mackenzie's schedule was nearly the same, and that suited them both just fine.

Morgan's new friend had been brought up with the school of thought that you had to earn money before you could spend it. As a result, she was not one for shopping sprees or running a credit card balance to the max. Morgan admired that.

Monday night, Morgan was surprised when her father arrived home early enough to take her out for dinner to a French restaurant near the hospital. She saw Cy only in passing when they got home.

Tuesday played out much the same. This time, Philip took her out to an Argentinean steak place in Oranjestad. The restaurant was packed, but they had a table waiting for them. The food was great, but the portions were gigantic. They came back home with enough left over to last them for a week. There was no sign of life in the guesthouse.

Morgan really missed seeing Cy, but it seemed that she and her father were finally breaking down the wall of ice between them. As she lay in bed, she thought about Philip. Their dinners were filled with conversation, and this surprised her. He appeared to be honestly interested in everything she did back in Boston, and even asked a lot of questions about Jean and her new husband. Morgan was mature enough not to harbor fanciful thoughts about any remnants of romance still lingering between the two. She understood that her father's interest was simply curiosity.

Wednesday morning, Morgan woke to an empty house. Outside her window, two annoying birds were singing arias to each other.

"Okay . . . okay," she murmured. "I'm up."

Coming out of the bathroom, she left her crutches by her bed and started toward the kitchen. On days like this, Morgan was impatient to have her cast off. For the first time since breaking her leg, she really wanted to try so many things. Now, she was counting the days until she'd get the darned thing off. So different from when she was in Boston. Thinking back now, she realized she'd just accepted the cast and the crutches as an inevitable part of her life.

Morgan felt different here. There were so many things to do. Places to go. People to meet. But—what to wear?

In Aruba, she thought, *you never see or hear weather reports.*

"Of course not, genius," she muttered. "The weather's always the same." Crossing the open area toward the kitchen, a door at the end of a short hallway caught her eye. The front door. She'd never used it. Going down the hall, she pulled the door open and stepped out.

There was a small veranda and a path leading to another gate to the street. The path was narrow and hemmed in on either side with green shrubs filled with yellow flowers. Six colorful little lizards and two iguanas were sitting on the path, eyeing her.

"Move along, you!" As she moved to shoo

them off, Morgan heard the door click shut behind her.

"Oh, great!" She tried the handle, but she already knew it would be locked.

No crutches, dressed only in a long T-shirt that ended mid-thigh, she made her way to the gate and peeked out at the street. It was deserted.

"Thank God for small favors."

Taking a deep breath, she limped as quickly as she could along the fence. Halfway to the gate, she saw a small landscaping truck filled with laborers coming down the street. The truck came rumbling by just as she got to the gate leading into the courtyard, and Morgan slipped inside to the sound of whistles and good-natured laughter behind her. In moments, the street was quiet again.

"Great, Morgan," she said, her back to the gate. "Put on a show, why don't you?"

She made her way to the sliding glass door. Locked. She looked around the veranda. There were a thousand places a key could be hidden, but Morgan didn't know if Philip even tucked one away out here for emergencies. She considered going to one of the neighbors' houses and asking to use the phone. She hadn't met any of them, and she looked at her reflection in the glass door. She wasn't really dressed for socializing.

Mackenzie wouldn't be coming by to pick her up for work, either. She'd told Morgan the day before that she had a doctor's appointment.

Morgan tried the windows facing the courtyard. They were all locked. She wasn't going to venture out onto the street again, that was for sure.

She looked across at the guesthouse. It was a long shot, but she didn't have many other choices. She hobbled over to Cy's place. The door was bolted. Walking around the building, she spotted another window overlooking the courtyard. Another step and Morgan could see it was unlocked.

To avoid getting cut, she had to work her way carefully between a couple of giant aloe bushes. As she pushed a large spike of the plant aside, she almost placed her bare foot on the tail of a two-foot-long iguana. The bright green lizard merely blinked at her and ambled off.

"Well, excuse me," she said to the retreating creature.

When she reached the window, she first pressed her face against the glass. It was his bedroom.

"Figures."

The bottom of the window was about chest high, and it stuck a little when she tried to push it up. A few huffs and puffs, and she knew it was this way from the humidity. She gave it one last shove, though, and was stunned when it suddenly shot up.

"Well, that wasn't so tough," she said, peering inside.

His bed was made and, with the exception of a T-shirt and some shorts on a chair, everything looked pretty neat. He had one picture frame on a bedside table, but she couldn't see who was in the picture from this angle. That was where she also spotted the phone. There was no way Morgan could reach it, though, where she was standing.

There was only one thing to do.

Morgan studied the size of the opening and decided it was smaller than the windows they had in their house back in Boston. She thought she could pass through it, though.

Standing on her cast, she tried to put her good leg in first. A couple of minutes of struggling sent home the message that either the window was about an inch too high or she was as stiff as a two-by-four. For some reason, she just couldn't get her legs to split the 180 degrees she needed them to go.

Going in headfirst seemed to be the only viable option. Morgan looked around her again, peering over the fence and hoping for some busybody neighbor that might be going by. A police cruiser would be nice, even. Maybe some good citizen walking by who might see it as their civic duty to call in to the authorities and report a breaking and entering in progress.

No such luck. The people were just too trusting around here.

"I'm going in," she whispered. Both hands went in first, and her head followed. Pulling herself up she was soon hanging half in and half out. Just as her fingers touched the tiled floor, she started sliding forward on her stomach. She definitely didn't have the flexibility of a gymnast, but she was proud of her snake impression. Her butt cleared. Walking forward on her hands, she cleared the thighs.

Her ankle only tapped the open window. It was the gentlest of taps, but it was all that was needed.

That window came down like a guillotine. She was stuck.

Morgan let out a loud profanity and looked over her shoulder. The window had come down on the backs of her knees, just above the cast, trapping her.

She couldn't believe it. There she was, suspended from the window, balancing her upper body on her hands. She couldn't have put herself in a more awkward position if she tried.

"Don't panic," she told herself. "Breathe. You can do without an asthma attack right now."

Morgan lowered herself onto her elbows. That was as far as she could go, and she was nearly upside down. There was no way she could turn around. The good news was that if the window gave out, the fall wasn't far enough to break another bone.

She tried to work her good leg through, but the cast took up too much space. There was no way. Next, she tried to push up the window with the back of her leg. That was a joke.

She banged her head a couple of times on the floor. She'd done it again. She'd got herself into another impossible position.

Morgan sighed. "Feeling sorry for yourself isn't going to help," she muttered.

She wasn't going to be stuck like this all day. She looked around the floor. A pair of old sneakers and flip-flops were under the bed. Reaching as far as she could, she managed to pull the sneakers to her. She put them aside, deciding it wouldn't make her feel any better to throw them against anything.

Her back was already aching. She moved her weight to one elbow and looked over her shoulder at the bedside table. Everything looked so giant, so out of reach. She now understood the perspective of a mouse. Or a lizard.

Morgan shuddered, looking around for any colorful creatures that might be hiding. She hadn't seen any indoors, but you never knew.

Thinking from that perspective actually helped.

Almost immediately, Morgan saw the phone wire coming out of the wall beneath the bed.

A bundle of it was bunched up and secured with a tie wrap. From there it ran up to the table and the phone.

She stretched as far as she could with one of the sneakers, but couldn't quite reach the phone line. Stuffing one sneaker inside the other, she tried again. The extension worked, and Morgan pulled the bunched wire within her reach. Once she had it, the rest was easy. She tugged on the wire until the phone crashed onto the floor and she yanked it over to her.

"A dial tone. Thank God," Morgan breathed as she put the handset to her ear. Wracking her brain, she remembered her father's work number. He'd only recited the number to her for the new cell phone speed dial on Sunday, but she was never happier than now that she had a good head for numbers.

Taking couple of deep breaths, Morgan dialed the number. It was his direct line. He sounded busy, but she could tell he was listening attentively when she explained that she'd locked herself out of the house. She kept her voice calm. She didn't think there was any point in mentioning the details of how and where she was stuck. She did mention, though, that she was able to get inside Cy's cottage and that was where she'd wait for him.

Well, most of her was inside, she thought.

Hanging up, she felt much better. All she had to do now was to find some way to entertain herself until her father got here.

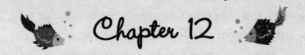

$\mathcal{L}$ess than a week ago Cy had been pretty annoyed that Philip Callahan hadn't wanted to spend any time with his daughter. Today, however, he had no problem taking a couple of hours off of work to run home and help Morgan get back inside the villa.

Cy knew Callahan was working at it. As much as the younger man missed not having any time with her, he understood this was probably the last chance these two might have to build any kind of father–daughter relationship.

Cy was in Bakval in fewer than twenty minutes. Coming in through the courtyard, he saw no sign of her. It surprised him a little, but he figured she was probably watching TV or reading a book in his place.

Aruba was a hundred times safer than D.C., but habit made him lock the front door to the guesthouse. Cy knew exactly how Morgan was able to get inside the cottage. He hated sleeping with the air-conditioning on, so he always left the bedroom window open at night. He closed it every morning, but he probably hadn't locked it.

He unlocked the door and went in.

"Hello? Morgan?"

"I need help."

Déjà vu all over again, he thought.

Dropping his keys on a little table by the door, he walked toward the bedroom.

"Morgan?"

"In here."

"What are you doing in there?"

"Stop asking questions. Just get in here and help me."

"You're not naked, are you?"

"Very funny."

He pushed open the door slowly, still not really knowing what to expect. The first thing he saw was her butt in the air. Her underwear had the Boston Red Sox logo on each cheek. She was dangling upside down from the window, her legs caught by the sash. The rest of her disappeared behind the bed. He walked around and stared in disbelief, trying all the while to hold back his laughter.

Her shirt had bunched around her chest and most of her back was exposed. It was a very nice back. And beautiful legs. He really liked the shape of her ass, too. She was hot. No doubt about it. There was only one thing about her that he didn't like.

"I don't approve of your choice of baseball teams."

She picked up her head, and he couldn't hold in his laughter any longer. She'd used the shoelaces from his sneakers to hold together a couple dozen braids she'd woven in her hair. She was scowling at him fiercely.

He tried to look serious. "Morgan, do you have any idea where those shoelaces have been?"

Cy was lucky he wasn't within reach or she would have hurt him.

Her neck ached when she looked up. Her back was frozen from being in this position, and he was totally entertained.

"Are you going to help me out of this or not?"

"Not before I take some photos for the family album . . . and the Internet."

Morgan winged one of his sneakers—less

the shoelace—at him. Unfortunately, she missed.

"Cyrus Reed, if you don't get me out of that window *this* minute . . . !"

He was still smiling as he came close. "Yeah? What?"

"You just wait."

"I'm real scared," he said teasingly.

"Cy!"

"Hold on. Hold on. I'm doing it." Putting one hand on the back of her thighs, he carefully opened the window with the other. His tone softened. "It's going to hurt getting down."

Her back felt like it was permanently molded into the arched position. And when he started lowering her legs, it did hurt a lot. He was right there, though, crouched on the floor next to her, massaging her lower back.

"Stay there. Try to stretch it slowly."

Morgan pressed her cheek against the tiled floor and pulled her knees slowly into her chest.

"I can't believe I did this. What an idiot."

He lifted the braids off her face and smiled down at her. "When you said you were accident-prone, you weren't kidding, were you?"

She shook her head. "Still having fun at my expense, huh?"

He put both hands up in self-defense and sat on the floor. "I'm not, really."

The smile reached his eyes. He was lying. But Morgan was too happy to be released from her medieval torture rack to complain too much. She knew she must have presented quite a picture.

"Why did my father have to send you?"

"You're not happy to see me? I'm happy to see *you*," he said in a light tone.

Morgan shook her head at him, like she didn't believe a word he said. She sat up and all the blood drained from her head.

"Here, why don't you lean against me?" he said, serious now. "Take your time getting up."

For the first time, Morgan really looked at him. He was wearing a dress shirt and long pants and a pair of loafers. No socks. As always, he looked and smelled wonderful. She didn't even want to think about how *she* looked. And her hair! At least she had a good excuse. Braiding it had kept her sane while she'd been waiting.

He scooted around her and put an arm

around her waist, pulling her back against his chest. He was leaning against the bed.

"Isn't that better?"

It's perfect, Morgan agreed, but she found her voice gone. He had that effect on her. He made her think about doing things she'd never done before. She tried to clear her head and find a safe subject to talk about.

"What do you have against the Red Sox?"

"I'm a Yankee fan."

"Too bad. And here, I thought I liked you."

His other hand slid across her stomach as he growled in her ear. "Are you saying you *don't* like me?"

"That's the problem." She half turned in his arms and looked into his green eyes. "Despite your bossiness, and being as slow as molasses in coming to my rescue, *and* the fact that you are so foolish in your choice of baseball teams . . . I like you a lot."

It was inevitable. He pushed her braids out of her face, and he kissed her.

This time was different than the last time. Morgan knew what to expect. She knew what she wanted. He tasted like mint and smelled like spice. As their mouths danced, she felt herself growing breathless. She threaded her fingers into his hair, encouraging him to deepen the kiss. When he slid his hand onto her breast, though, she caught his wrist and tore her mouth free.

"Don't, Cy. Not yet."

He sat still for a moment, his forehead resting against hers for a couple of seconds. Then he caressed her hair, placed a kiss on the bridge of her nose. He cupped her face and looked into her eyes.

"You know I like you, Morgan. I'm . . . well, very attracted to you. And you're right. This situation is way too comfortable. It's too easy for us to get carried away. I know that."

She nodded.

"We can take it slower. Any way you want to go. Whatever speed. Remember, though, I'm just a guy."

"I know," Morgan replied. She didn't want to be a tease. "Cy, I feel more comfortable with you than anyone else I've met in a long time—maybe ever. But it's only been six days."

"Not six days. Fifteen years. You cast your spell on me that long ago."

She smiled. "The skinny-dipping did it, huh?"

"You got it. But of course, this hair is what knocked me off my feet today." He raised the shoelaces and looked critically at her braiding job.

"You're making fun of me again."

"Me? Never." He got up, pulling her to her feet.

Morgan truly appreciated what he was doing for her. Giving her the choice. Not getting mad at her and walking out . . . the way Jack did.

It was an impulsive gesture, but she didn't care. She wrapped her arms around him and gave him an affectionate hug. "Thank you."

He returned the hug, molding her to him. "But I can't do it alone. You have to help."

She pressed her palms on his chest and looked into his eyes. "How?"

He shook his head and smiled. "You don't even realize it, Morgan, but you're incredibly hot."

"I am not," she said with a laugh.

"Don't argue. Just take notes."

"Yes, sir."

"No standing around naked in your bathroom and asking me to come in."

"I didn't do that on purpose!" Morgan said, starting to explain but then deciding against it. "Deal."

"No walking around the villa in a skimpy T-shirt and your underwear."

"I was wearing a robe," she said in her own defense.

He gave her the look again.

"Fine. Fine. I'll wear my nun's habit when I know you're coming over."

"And no climbing through the window of my bedroom. You can use the door."

She punched him in the chest, but didn't move out of the circle of his arms. "You're making it sound like I had an ulterior motive."

"The problem is, whatever motive you had, I'm happy to buy into it. So, if you want me to keep my hands to myself, then don't do it."

"Anything else, mighty lawgiver?"

He nodded. "The hair. This new style really does it for me. Especially the shoelaces. There's something very raw and primitive about it. It makes me want to—"

"That's it. You've really lost it. It must be

too much Aruban sun. I knew it wasn't good for you, but I never thought it caused brain damage." She took him by the arm and started toward the door. "By the way, you better have a key to the villa because I have to get ready to go to work."

"And if I don't have a key?"

"It's on your key chain. I've seen it." She grabbed the keys by the door and stepped out into the courtyard. She pointed to the two likely candidates. "It's one of these two."

"How about if neither one works?"

He was daring her, teasing. She stood facing him on the brick pathway, meeting his challenge. "Then I guess all bets will be off. I'll have to spend the rest of the summer in the guesthouse looking like this."

Morgan shrieked as he snatched the keys out of her hand and threw them over his shoulder.

"You're on."

Chapter 13

It took some prodding, but Morgan convinced Cy to wait around until she got ready so that he could drop her off at the restaurant.

The incident at home was not easy to shake off, though. Sitting on a stool at the cash register, she could still feel his strong arms around her. She could still feel his hand on her waist. The morning passed in a kind of a haze. Morgan added up checks and counted out change and ran credit cards through, but all the while her mind kept drifting back to that little bedroom in the guesthouse.

Mac arrived at work around noon, and right away, Morgan knew there was something on her friend's mind. Around 2:30, the restaurant emptied, so the two of them grabbed a couple of sodas and went to sit at one of the curbside tables.

"Can I ask you something?" Mackenzie said when they were seated.

"Of course."

"Are you on anything?" Mac asked in a whisper.

"You mean, drugs?" Morgan asked, a little perplexed.

"No."

"For my leg?"

Mackenzie laughed. She leaned forward and asked more quietly, "Are you on the pill?"

"Oh, birth control."

For a couple of seconds, Morgan tried to imagine if there was any way Mackenzie had talked to Cy about what had happened this morning. She quickly dismissed it, though.

"No," she finally answered.

"Then . . ." Mac hesitated. "How do you make sure . . . ?"

"I wear a chastity belt," Morgan replied in a confidential tone. "It's state-of-the-art, titanium-plated, and comes with high-frequency sensors and digital locks that are only set to open sometime after 2010."

"Wow."

"And if that fails, I still wield a mean crutch." She picked one up and waved it around. "They're multipurpose and pretty handy."

Mac smiled. "I'm serious."

"I don't do it."

"No sex?"

"Not yet," Morgan answered honestly.

"You've got to be tempted sometimes. I mean, isn't everyone?"

She never had been. Not seriously. Not before today.

"I suppose. I guess I always figured I'd start thinking about it when I found myself feeling seriously tempted." Which meant, Morgan realized, she should be giving it some serious thought starting now. She looked carefully at her friend. "Why do you ask?"

"Because . . . well, like you, I've never been . . . pulled in that direction. But I've started thinking about it already. This summer." Mac glanced over her shoulder in the direction of the kitchen, making sure no one was eavesdropping. "Boys have always treated me like one of the guys. I never had to deal with it, really. But that was before Nick."

"You and Nick are . . . involved?"

"Kind of. And he wants to go out with me again. No running into each other someplace with friends. He's asked me out on a real date. Friday night." Mackenzie rubbed at a nonexistent stain on the table. Her eyes were huge and full of emotion when she looked up at Morgan. "And I still can't believe it. Nick Bloch. Ever since he arrived in Aruba, I've felt this crazy crush for him. But I didn't know if he felt that way about me. At first, I think he just saw me as a friend for windsurfing. But something happened during this past week. It's different now."

"That's great," Morgan replied enthusiastically.

Her friend looked doubtful. "I don't know. I mean, he has everything—looks, college, a great future, a family that he loves."

Morgan put a hand on top of Mac's. "Don't sell yourself short. You have a lot going for you, too. You're a catch."

Mackenzie smiled in gratitude but shook her head. "I'm just me—half a family, no awareness whatsoever about style, or what's in and what's out. I'm not like the Lizards. I don't really even know how I'm supposed to be with a guy that I'm attracted to. I've never been a game player. I don't know how to be coy . . . or sexy . . . or whatever. I have no finesse."

"Well, that makes the two of us, then. But I

think all of that is definitely overrated."

Mac smiled. "But don't you think it's amazing that someone like Nick would want to go out with me? I mean, look at me. I'm tall, dark, thin, flat—this is not exactly Beyoncé's body here. And with this hair, I can't tell you how many times people have mistaken me for a boy."

"Then those people must have been blind. Nick isn't. You're beautiful. More important, you're genuinely a good person, and that counts a heck of a lot more than that other stuff." Morgan leaned forward, whispering now. "You were asking all those questions about birth control. You two haven't already . . . ?"

Mackenzie shook her head. "Saturday night, we came close. We almost got carried away in the car when I was dropping him off. Almost. But I asked him to stop. And he did."

Another check in the plus column for Nick, Morgan thought.

"He said he'd take care of things. When the time was right. When I was ready. But I can't let it go at that. I know that's not enough. So I went to this doctor today. She put me on the pill."

"They won't take effect immediately. You still have to be careful." Although Morgan hadn't been sexually involved with anyone yet, she'd had plenty of speeches from her mother. Jean was obsessive about sex education. Morgan remembered getting "the talk" for the first time when she was still in elementary school.

"I know. I've had plenty of sex education classes at school . . . and a few hints now and then from my mother. I know teenagers here are supposed to be miles ahead of American kids in these things," Mackenzie said. "But I'm not. Maybe I'm a defect, but I really didn't have anyone else that I could talk to about this except you. I mean, you're the only female friend that I've had in a long time."

"I'm glad you did."

"So you think I'm doing the right thing?"

Tough question, Morgan thought. Even as she sat looking at her new friend, she knew that this was one of those moments when what she said really mattered. But what did she really know about it?

"Look, Mac," she started. "I'm not any wiser about this stuff than you. What I focus on is keeping my life as simple as I can and protecting myself. If you think going on the pill is going to help, then I say go for it. You still need to protect yourself from STDs, but pregnancy should definitely be avoided. Does that make any sense?"

"Very."

"You just finished high school. You'll be going to college somewhere away from the island, right?"

"Yeah?"

"Well, that's another world out there. A world you need to be prepared for. I think you're smart for doing it. Even if it doesn't work out with Nick, you're thinking ahead."

Mackenzie squeezed Morgan's hand. "You're right. Thanks."

Neither of them saw the silver Mercedes until it had pulled up to the curb near their table and honked its horn. The Lizards were inside, looking good as always. Kate was on the passenger side in the front seat, and her window came down smoothly.

"Mac, Megan. What have you two been up to?"

"It's Morgan," Mac said, correcting her.

"Right. Didn't I say Morgan?" Kate responded innocently. "Sorry. So where have you two been hiding?"

"We've been working," Mac said. "How about you guys?"

Kate started to tell them about a scuba diving trip they'd gone on yesterday at one of the many wrecks in the waters around Aruba. A taxi pulled up behind the Mercedes and the driver honked the horn loudly. Morgan could see they'd partially blocked the road. Ellie was behind the wheel, and she waved the driver to go around her. As he went around, they could see him scowling and muttering, and Morgan thought about how a Boston driver would have responded. Not quite so politely, she decided.

"Anyway," Kate was saying to Morgan. "Have you seen Cy around?"

"Yeah. We live in the same villa." It didn't sound quite the way she'd wanted it to, but so what?

"Do you know what time he gets home from work?"

Morgan shook her head. "Not really. It's different every day."

"Are his phone and answering machine working?"

Morgan didn't know about the answering machine. "I used his phone this morning."

"That's funny . . ." Kate paused, and Morgan had a pretty good idea that there might be an unanswered message.

"Do you have his work number?" Kate asked.

Morgan shook her head again. No way was she giving that up.

Another car pulled up behind the Mercedes, beeping its horn loudly. This time, Beth poked her head out the back window, yelling to the driver to go around.

"Well, we're throwing a party Saturday night at my house. Can you tell Cy that I expect him to come around in the afternoon to help us set up?"

"I'll tell him," Morgan replied as pleasantly as she could.

"Thanks," Kate said, smiling sweetly. One of the Lizards whispered something from the backseat. "Oh, and we'd love to have the two of you come over, too. About eight. Bring whatever you want to drink."

"Thanks," Mac said, keeping a smile pasted on until the Mercedes pulled away. "There's going to be talk about us."

"Talk about what?"

"We were holding hands, and they saw it." Mackenzie gave her a knowing nod. "I'm not girlie enough for them. They're sure I'm gay."

Morgan sat back and smiled. "So, they think you've found yourself a playmate?"

"They can think whatever they want," Mac said. "In fact, maybe it's a good thing."

"Why is that?"

"Kate didn't seem as threatened by you, in case you didn't notice. They even invited us to their party. You'd still better watch your back, though."

"Will you go?"

"Will you?"

Morgan thought about that for a couple of seconds and then shook her head. "I don't know. Last Friday they were pretty determined to make me stay away from Cy. I don't like that."

"Things have progressed since then, haven't they? With him, I mean."

"Somewhat." Morgan shrugged, but couldn't

hold back a smile. "I'm not into any competition thing, though. I can't go there and pretend it won't bother me if Kate is all over him."

"Maybe he won't want to go."

"Maybe, but I don't really know that, either. We're nowhere near where you and Nick are. Whatever time we've spend together has been . . . well, coincidental, I guess. Because of my father. And because we live so close. We don't have any attachments."

"I think you're wrong about that. And I think you're wrong about not going to that party. You should go. Let Cy show everybody—including Kate—who he's interested in."

That would require serious mojo, and Morgan wasn't sure she had enough.

Chapter 14

The cashier who took over from her for the dinner shift was running late, so Morgan stayed at the restaurant until 7:00. Mackenzie was doing an extra shift that night, too, so Morgan called for a taxi to take her the embarrassingly short distance to the villa.

Philip's and Cy's cars were both in the driveway, and Morgan noticed that the lights of the guesthouse were on as she came in through the courtyard. She thought about when the best time would be to pass on Kate's message about the party.

Never, Morgan answered herself. Still, she knew she would. *If* she saw him.

She heard the shower running in her father's bathroom when she came in. She called a greeting but doubted Philip heard it. The phone rang, and she leaned her crutches against the sofa and answered it. It was Cy.

"How was your day?"

"Uneventful."

"I saw you come in."

She felt the thrill ripple up her spine at his words. She was ridiculous.

"And you didn't come out to greet me?"

"You were armed with those two deadly weapons. Hey, I hear Philip has something going on tonight. Do you want to do a dinner and a movie?"

The way he said it, Morgan couldn't help but wonder if the invitation was because of her father's prodding. She felt her ego deflate. Still, seeing a movie was harmless, so either way it was okay.

"That'd be great. What's playing? And what time?"

"I didn't know if you'd be up for it, so I haven't checked, yet."

"Do you have a phone number for the theater? I can call and check for us."

"Let me look in the phone book."

While he was searching for the number, Morgan got up and reached for the pad of paper on the counter. The tip of the pencil next to it was broken.

The water in the bathroom had stopped running. Morgan looked around the counter and didn't see anything else to write with. The door to Philip's office was open, and his briefcase was sitting on the desk. She went in, pad of paper in hand, and grabbed a pen from a cup holder on the desk. She sat down on the chair.

"I'm ready when you are."

"Just a second. For an island this small, they have a huge phone book."

Morgan looked around the office, realizing this was the first time she'd been inside it. The first thing she noticed was that there were no windows. Other than that, the room was of average size, about the same dimensions as her bedroom. Two bookcases, one file cabinet, the desk and chair. One other chair and three large, framed Caribbean posters completed the furnishings.

Her father definitely didn't seem to go in for clutter. There were no piles of newspapers. No files or papers scattered around.

Even the desk was pretty neat. Aside from his closed briefcase, a laptop sat on one end. She eyed that. It felt like ages since she'd checked her e-mail. But she didn't have time for that now. Beneath a green-shaded desk lamp, a cup holder contained an assortment of pens and pencils. There was only one framed picture peeking from behind the briefcase. She reached over to see what it was.

It was a baby picture of her. Chubby face, a big smile, only four teeth, short curly red hair and bright blue eyes. Cake was smeared all over her face and clothes. Her mother had a copy of this one, too. It was of Morgan's first birthday. The story behind it was that instead of waiting for the cake to be cut for the guests, she'd climbed onto the table and sat in the middle of it.

Morgan smiled. She remembered what Cy had told her about seeing more of her pictures. So Philip must have some at work, too.

"Ready?"

"Shoot," she answered, putting the frame back.

Cy rattled off the number. "Whatever you decide will be fine with me. There are a couple of places around the movie theater, so we can grab something to eat in town."

"Sounds great."

"I'll be over after I take a quick shower."

"Okay," she said, hanging up.

Morgan dialed the number of the theater, but the line was busy. She sat back in the chair and decided to wait and try again in another minute. The middle drawer of the desk was open a little. She noticed there was a key that had been left in the drawer lock. Without even thinking about it, she slid the drawer open.

The drawer was neat, too, but what caught her eye was a U.S. passport on the left. The gold embossed lettering on the navy blue cover gleamed in the light of the desk lamp. She was ready to slide the drawer shut when she realized the passport was sitting on top of several others.

"What the heck?" she murmured.

There were five of them in all. She picked them up and looked at the passports. All different colors. From five different countries.

Morgan glanced quickly at the door of the office. Suddenly, a sick feeling settled in the pit of her stomach. She hesitantly opened the blue passport with the American eagle so prominently displayed.

The first page contained her father's picture. But not his real name.

She stared at it in confusion. Her hands were

shaking when she opened a brown-colored passport. Venezuela. Philip's picture. And again, a different name.

She quickly stacked the passports in the drawer the way she'd found them and closed it as her father's bedroom door opened.

"Morgan? That you?"

Her heart pounded in her chest. He hadn't told her that his office was off-limits, so she stayed where she was and pressed the REDIAL button on the phone. It was still busy, but she held the phone to her ear as her father appeared in the doorway.

"Checking movie times," she said.

His hair was still wet. He was wearing a formal dress shirt and black pants with a black satin stripe down the side. Working on a bow tie, he came into the room.

She took the phone away from her ear and punched the OFF button. "The line is busy."

"I'm sorry about abandoning you yet again."

"No problem."

He was looking at her curiously. "I found out at the last minute that I have to put in an appearance at some shindig at the Governor's Mansion."

Morgan nodded, but all the while her stomach was turning and twisting as she searched for a reasonable explanation for the passports. He just *couldn't* be doing something illegal. The itch down inside her cast was back, and she couldn't do a thing about it.

"That's okay," she replied. "Things happen."

He reached over and put his briefcase on the floor. She saw his gaze make a quick sweep of the top of the desk.

"I hope it's okay with you," he said, "but I made a doctor's appointment for you at the hospital on Monday. I figured it'd be good to go and meet the orthopedist a few days before they take your cast off. Just in case they need any information from Boston."

"Sure. That'd be great," Morgan responded, trying to sound cheerful.

Philip was doing responsible things. He was doing his job as a parent. The weird thing was that this hurt her even more.

What a mess, she thought.

She didn't want to start liking him now . . . not if he was getting himself into trouble. The emotions were welling up in her eyes, and she had to put a stop to it before she embarrassed herself. She redialed the number.

"Busy again." She grabbed the piece of paper with the phone number on it and got up.

"So I guess Cy asked you about a movie and dinner?"

She nodded. So it had been Philip's idea, after all. Morgan went by him, and he followed her out of the office.

"By the way," she asked, turning to face him. "Why do you lock this office?"

He stared at her for a full two seconds. "Well, work. Lots of times I bring home classified documents. So it's a security issue."

"I'm not into stealing state secrets."

"I don't lock it because of you. It's because anyone could break into this place if they want to. A few flimsy window locks aren't going to keep a burglar out. I guess I just want to make it more difficult for them."

"You have something worth stealing in there?"

"No," he laughed. "I guess I'm just being cautious, but it's really more just my routine."

Morgan looked at him for a long moment. If he wasn't going to tell her, then she wasn't going to ask . . . not now, anyway.

"These locks are anything but flimsy," she said finally. "Trust me, I was on the outside, trying to get in this morning. It was impossible."

"I'm sorry about that. Maybe tomorrow we could figure out a good hiding place for a key."

She nodded again. "I think I'll go and change."

"By the way, how did I do?" he asked, meaning with his tie.

Morgan looked at his handiwork. It needed a little adjustment. She reached up to straighten it and once again a riptide of emotions started taking her under.

She hated this. She didn't want to be in the middle of trouble. She wanted him to be okay, to be doing the right thing. Maybe it was from watching too many spy movies, but she was imagining the worst possible scenarios.

Still, she loved him. He was her father. Shit.

"You look like a hundred bucks."

"You mean a hundred florins?"

"I haven't exchanged any money yet. It seems like everyone takes the dollar."

"That's true."

He started to turn away, but then on impulse, she decided to ask him about the passports. "In your office, I saw —"

The knock on the glass door stopped her. He looked at her closely for a second before they both turned to the door. Philip waved Cy in.

Morgan tucked the question away and shook her head in disbelief at Cy. He was wearing a New York Yankees T-shirt over khaki cargo shorts.

"You were saying?" Philip was looking steadily at her. "In the office, you saw what?"

"What? Oh . . . my baby picture. The one of my messy face. I didn't know you had that."

He smiled. "That's a special picture. In fact, I have another copy of it on my desk at work. It's so *you*. You had a knack for getting into trouble back then. If it wasn't mischief, it was always something you were getting into."

"I'm glad I grew out of that," Morgan said, casting a warning glance at Cy. It was obvious Philip didn't know about her being stuck in the guesthouse window this morning. "I'll be ready in a minute."

"Were you able to get any information on the movies and times?"

"The line was busy." She tossed him the phone. "I have to change. I'll be right out."

"You don't have to dress too fancy."

"Don't worry, I won't. But I do have to put on something to balance out the embarrassment you're wearing."

Chapter 15

Morgan wore her official Red Sox game shirt over jean shorts. Leaving the house, she could see the amusement on her father's face as he watched them go. Cy waited until they were driving away from the villa before he made any comment about her choice of clothes.

"You know, I think we have to stop and buy you an Aruba T-shirt."

Morgan twisted in the seat and pointed to a Red Sox logo on the back pocket of her jeans. "Did you see this?"

Hands on the wheel, he took a quick glance and made a face. "That's sick. I suppose you're still wearing those horrendous underpants, too?"

She shook her head. "No, I changed into a gray pair that I only wear for away games. I also have a matching tank top under this shirt. And this little border on my socks."

"What are you trying to do, make me leave you at the theater after the movie?"

"Hey, you're the one who said I shouldn't look or dress sexy around you. I just figured I'd be safe wearing my ultimate fan uniform."

"Unfortunately, that's totally illogical."

"Don't tell me this is a turn-on for you."

He shook his head from side to side. "The problem is that I look at you and start thinking of ways to get you *out* of those ugly clothes."

Morgan patted her bag and smiled. "Then it's a good thing I brought along my handy Red Sox bobble-head doll."

He was having difficulty keeping a straight face. "Which player?"

"David Ortiz. I should tell you, though, that I really would have brought along my Johnny Damon doll if it had arrived before I left Boston. But Big Papi will do just fine if I have to fight you off."

"I love a challenge," he said, swerving onto the shoulder and slamming on the breaks.

"What are you doing?"

"Showing you how ineffective those Red Sox players are at keeping this Yankee fan from what he's been thinking about all day."

Pulling her into his arms, Cy kissed her . . . long and hard. When he pulled back, she was not thinking of anything but how much she'd missed the feeling of his arms around her.

"And what do you have to say about that?"

She struggled but found her voice. "I should have waited for my Johnny Damon doll."

Cy's laughter rang out. Throwing the car in gear, he pulled back on the road. Morgan smiled and enjoyed the tingly feeling that was running all over her body. He said he'd been thinking about her all day.

They reached the outskirts of Oranjestad in ten minutes. The streets were just coming alive with nighttime window-shoppers, diners, and partyers.

"What were the movies and what times?" she asked.

"I ended up talking to your father, so I didn't get a chance to call back. How about if we just go down there and improvise?"

"Sounds great. Whatever," Morgan said happily. She immediately grew serious. Now that he'd mentioned her father, she saw a window of opportunity and decided to go for it. "Cy, what *exactly* does my father do?"

He glanced at her curiously. "You don't know?"

"I know he's an accountant and that he works for the Department of Energy. But other than that, I really don't have a clue. What's he doing in Aruba?"

Cy explained to her about the recent acquisition by a U.S. company of Aruba's oil refinery at the southern end of the island. He said her father's assignment here had something to do with that.

Morgan tried to figure how the five passports she'd seen could have anything to do with his job tracking oil imports.

Thoughts of her father as an international terrorist, preparing to sabotage the refinery, just didn't fit into her image of him. He was an accountant, for God's sake, not James Freaking Bond!

"Do you think he's happy with his job?"

"I don't know." Cy's eyes were glued to the traffic. "Why do you ask?"

"I guess I was thinking that if I had to do without him being around for all these years, I want to know that he got some satisfaction out of his career."

Cy pulled the car into a parking space by the Seaport Marina. The lights from the casino beyond the boat slips reflected on the black water.

"I'm sure he did. So did my father. But I think, for some people, the excitement inevitably starts to wear off at some point. That happened in my family. That's why my father had to try something totally new. It could be that the same thing is happening to Philip."

Pieces of a puzzle were starting to fall into place. The problem was, Morgan didn't think she was going to like the picture. "What do you mean?"

Cy switched off the engine and the headlights. They sat there looking at the harbor ahead of them.

"I can't put my finger on it exactly. It's just . . . he doesn't like to spend a lot of time behind a desk. He is always running somewhere. There are a lot of phone calls. For an accountant, he doesn't seem real excited about crunching numbers, doing reports. All that stuff. His attention is somewhere else, supposedly on some project that I don't know anything about."

This didn't make her feel better. Something was definitely going on.

"So should we go and see what's playing?" he asked her.

"Sure," Morgan said, stepping out of the car.

Cy came around and fetched her crutches from the backseat and handed it to her. "How many more days?"

"Eight." The laughter of a group of girls walking along the street reminded Morgan of what she had forgotten to tell him. "Oh, the Lizards stopped by the restaurant today. Kate wanted me to tell you that they are having a party—"

"I already know about it. She left four phone messages and one handwritten note taped to the guesthouse door."

They walked toward the movie theater. He hadn't returned Kate's messages. Morgan didn't know what to say. She did know how to feel about it, though. *Great!*

"I've explained things to her over and over. That day we ran into them at the Natural Bridge, I spelled it out again on the way to the restaurant in Santa Cruz. I told her we're history. But she doesn't get it."

Morgan had been dumped the day before

her junior prom, but she'd never tried to hang on to Jack. Except for a few initial tears, Morgan realized she had hardly looked back. Of course, Jack and Cy were entirely different.

"So what are you going to do about it?" Cy asked, breaking into her thoughts.

"Me?"

"You," he repeated.

She came to a stop in the middle of the parking lot and looked at him in confusion. "Report a gang of blonde bimbettes stalking the villa?"

"That's a good start." He said. "But the Aruban police won't do anything about it."

"How about if I beat Kate with a crutch?"

He seemed to consider that for a few seconds longer, but then shook his head. "I have a better idea."

"I'm all ears."

"We'll tell her what's going on between us."

Morgan admired the play of the wind in his hair. "Okay. But don't you think you should tell *me* what's going on between us? I mean, when we tell Kate, we probably want to be on the same page."

He laughed softly. "Let's bag the movie."

"What do you want to do?"

"Let's sit and talk."

"Okay."

Cy pointed to a bench about twenty feet from them, facing the harbor. They walked over to it and sat down.

"I do expect to be fed, though, before we go back."

Cy took her crutches and moved them a safe distance away. He put an arm around Morgan's shoulder and nestled her against him.

A light, balmy breeze caressed her arms, and the smell of the sea and flowers mingled with his cologne and filled her senses. The stars were bright in the black silk sky, and the sound of steel drum music was coming from somewhere along the harbor front. She took a deep breath, wondering how she ever got here . . . sitting under a tropical night sky on an island paradise with a truly amazing guy's arm around her.

Cy finally broke the comfortable silence. "Morgan, how would you describe our relationship?"

"Let's see . . . one based solidly on obligation?"

"What?"

"You've been stuck with chauffeuring me around because you work for my father."

"That was last Thursday. How would you describe it, starting Friday?"

"Guilt."

"How do you figure that?"

"You saw my naked butt in the bathroom," Morgan explained. "You feel guilty because I have no tan line."

He laughed. "You are a piece of work."

"Why, thank you."

Cy lifted her chin until he was looking into her eyes. "Are you nervous, Morgan?"

"Maybe."

"Why?"

"Because I'm a Callahan . . . and talking like this is not our strongest family trait."

"Okay, then I'll do the talking." Lights from the casino sparkled in his eyes. "I think we have something very special going on between us."

"You do?"

"Yeah, I do. We speak the same language. That's more than I've ever had with anybody else before. I love spending time with you, talking to you, kissing you, arguing over your complete lack of understanding about baseball teams." His thumb caressed her cheek. "So what do you say?"

"About what?"

His hand cupped the back of her head. He brought her mouth close to his. "Say we're an item. Say you'll go out with me."

She smiled and nodded. Their noses rubbed. He stole a kiss from her lips.

"I'm not very good at sharing, though," she said. "You should probably know that up front."

"I'm not, either."

"I may have to put Kate and the Lizards in their place."

"We'll do that together," he told her, stealing another kiss. "My guess is that we could come up with a pretty good plan."

"I'm invited to their party on Saturday. How would you like to go as my date?"

He laughed. "I like your style."

And Morgan liked his. Wrapping her arms around his neck, she drew his face to hers and showed him.

Chapter 16

Morgan figured it would be best all the way around if she just told her father about the new development between her and Cy. As usual, he didn't get home until late that night, though, and only poked his head into her room long enough to say he had another last-minute day trip that he had to make off the island tomorrow.

He was gone by the time she woke up the next morning.

That was fine with Morgan, though. She had a mission. She needed to find out what was going on.

She glanced out across the courtyard at the guesthouse. No sign of Cy. Morgan knew he'd be coming over for breakfast before going to work, so she took a quick shower and got dressed.

After their talk last night, Morgan knew they'd be walking a fine line regarding how physical their relationship would get. She was as tempted as he was, but they both wanted to take their time. At least, she did. And that meant no temptations.

Leaving her bedroom, she noticed that the office door was locked. She wasn't discouraged, though, and decided to search Philip's bedroom.

One thing was certain to Morgan. Her mother hadn't divorced Philip because he was a slob. Everything in the bedroom was immaculate, pretty much like the rest of the house. Of course, she knew some of that was due to the efforts of their housekeeper, Clotilde. Morgan had met her in passing last Monday and was amazed at the whirlwind of energy the woman was.

Philip's bedroom was larger than hers. It contained the usual assortment of furniture, bed and side tables, lamps, two bureaus, an oversized reading chair, and an armoire that she guessed housed a television.

She checked the bureaus. One was empty. She turned her attention to the other. Shirts, underwear, socks. She felt around under the clothes, looking under the bottoms and at the backs of the drawers, remembering what she'd seen in movies about guns or keys being hidden there.

Nothing.

The double-wide closet was her next target. Rows of suits and jackets and pressed pants and shirts hung tidily on the metal bars. Everything was in its place.

She glanced up at the two rows of shelves above the hanging clothes. Stacked on them were an assortment of suitcases, light sweaters, and a couple of neatly folded blankets. One medium-sized file box sat on the upper shelf, and Morgan fixed her eyes on it. The top of it was slightly askew, like Philip might have reached in there recently.

She had to see what was in it.

Morgan's fingers could barely reach it. She gently started pulling. The avalanche came without warning.

Following the mysterious box, suitcases, sweaters, blankets—and the shelves they were sitting on—all came crashing down on top of her, knocking her to the floor. Thankfully the box was light, because it hit Morgan squarely on the head before all the contents dumped out on the floor around her.

Morgan stared in disbelief at hundreds of

airline barf bags scattered on her lap and on the floor.

"Are you okay?"

Startled, Morgan looked up. Cy stood in the doorway of the bedroom dressed for work.

"Oh, hi. When did you come in?"

"Just now. I heard the demolition crew working in here." He smiled, taking in the full extent of the disaster. "So . . . how's it going?"

"He collects barf bags."

He started laughing. "Hey, it's better than collecting Red Sox memorabilia."

"That's it. You're in trouble." She hauled herself to her feet and started toward him. "I'm going to give you a good bruising and put an end to all those wisecracks."

He met her in the middle of the bedroom and, before she could hurt him, pulled her into his arms, and sealed her lips with a kiss. She leaned into him, losing herself in his taste and touch. His hand moved down her back and gathered her so close against his body that there wasn't a breath of air between them.

"I like this kind of bruising," he said softly.

"There's more where that came from." She

smiled, kissing him again. "Oh . . . and good morning."

"I think we need to add sundresses to the 'too hot to wear' list," he said, pushing one strap of her dress down over her shoulder and pressing his lips to her skin.

Never mind the dress, his mouth was hot, and she loved the sensation. "I'm gradually running out of clothes I can wear."

"That's the idea." He ran his hands down over the curve of her bottom and pulled her closer against him. She didn't move away. She felt a thrill race to her very center.

He seemed to gather his self-control, looking over at the mess.

"So what happened here?" he asked.

"The shelves attacked me."

"You probably provoked them."

"Maybe a little." She hated to have Philip come home to this. "Will you help me fix it?"

"Of course!"

He left her standing in the middle of the room and went to test the brackets in the closet. They looked secure. He reached for one of the shelves that had fallen down. "What were you looking for?"

Morgan contemplated telling Cy about the passports, but decided against it. She felt so horrible thinking that Philip might be doing something wrong, committing a crime. At the same time, she didn't want to lie.

"I wanted to see what was inside this box," she said, crouching down on the floor and starting to put all the barf bags back inside of it. "I hope he didn't have his collection organized alphabetically by airline. Hey, look . . . Flugfelag Islands Air."

"That's great. But why were you in here?"

"Curiosity, okay? I was snooping around Philip's closet. I'm trying to . . . to understand him."

He paused with the shelf in hand. Their gazes met over the mess between them. "I know what you're going through."

Morgan doubted it, but she didn't say anything.

"You and Philip are doing a lot better . . . and in a lot less time . . . than my dad and I did."

"When was that?"

"Six years ago. I was fourteen and full of hormones and resentment and distrust. I really ran him through the wringer until I smartened up."

"So you were the one that had to change?"

He placed one end of the shelf on the floor and leaned on the other end.

"I don't know. I guess he changed, too. He wasn't only dealing with me. He was trying to kickstart his marriage with my mother again. And then there was my younger brother, the know-it-all of the family. For me, I just had to accept the fact that he was back, and this time he was going to stay. In the end, it was a heck of a lot better to have him back with us."

Morgan carefully placed the last of the barf bags in the box and put on the lid.

"I don't have all that. Philip *isn't* back. He *doesn't* care about his family. He was stuck with me for the summer because of my mother." She let out a frustrated breath. "At the same time, I can see that he's trying. There are moments when I really enjoy being with him. I like hearing him laugh. Tell stories. I can see myself in his eyes. Still, it hurts because I know it's just for a short time. Again."

Cy left the shelf on the floor and came over and took Morgan into his arms. The darn tears were threatening to fall again. She fought them.

"It's different now than when you were a

kid, though," he told her softly. "You don't need him. You can be friends. You can work things out on your own terms. You can enjoy the time you have with him, without worrying about what might or might not happen."

"Maybe," she replied, thinking again of the passports in the desk.

"He was nervous before you got here, Morgan. But I can tell you he's very happy that you're here now. I wouldn't write him off yet. Give him a chance."

"I am," she said, wiping at a runaway tear on her cheek.

"And I think he's almost at the end of these crazy hours and trips off-island, too. He keeps saying he's in the last throes of this project he's working on. He told me he'd have a lot more time, after he's done with it."

"What's the project?"

"You got me. But he was definite that the end's in sight." He cupped her face and placed a kiss on her forehead. "So hang in there."

She nodded, resigned to squash her curiosity for now. Maybe her father *was* doing the right thing. Maybe.

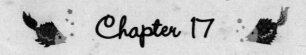

Chapter 17

They had everything back in the closet by the time Mackenzie arrived to pick Morgan up for work. Cy had called in earlier, telling someone at the office that he was running late. He told Morgan that he'd make up the work at the other end of the day. He wasn't worried about it.

On the way to the restaurant, Mac asked Morgan if she'd like to hang out and run a couple of errands with her tomorrow. Both of them had Friday off.

"Sure, what kind of errands?"

"I was hoping you'd help me pick out a dress."

Morgan smiled. "That's right. Tomorrow night is your big date with Nick."

"Not *big* date. It's only a date," Mac corrected. "I can't build this up too much. I don't want the 'big date' to turn out to be 'big disaster.'"

"Do you know where he's taking you?"

"We're going on one of those dinner-and-dance boats. It goes out of the harbor at Oranjestad."

"That sounds like a lot of fun," Morgan said. "I'm so happy for you."

Mac beamed. "I was also wondering if you'd want to do a half day at a spa at the Radisson. My mom knows the manager, and she can get us a huge discount."

"Wow, I've never done that."

"I can try to schedule us in for tomorrow morning."

"What do we do? Get a massage?"

"Massage, a facial, whatever. I'm definitely going to get someone to help with this hair. But you can get a body wrap, or even a mani-cure and pedicure, if you want."

"Count me in." Morgan thought it would be fun, and the discount would be especially nice since she was planning to pay for it herself. This was starting to feel like a real vacation.

They were still hammering out the details when Mackenzie pulled into the parking lot next to the restaurant. Right away, Morgan noticed the black Jaguar with tinted windows. It was parked at the very end of the lot, close to the street. Next to it, she could see a black stretch limo. A slick-looking guy, maybe in his twenties, and two gorilla-sized men who could have been ex–football players were standing between the two cars, chatting and keeping an eye on things. The gorillas were wearing matching black shirts and pants. *Probably on the same team*, she thought.

As much as the limo was an attention-getter, it was the Jaguar that caught Morgan's eye. She looked around and saw him just sitting down at a table outside the restaurant. Her good friend Porcupine Butt. He was sitting by the road, at the same table Mackenzie and Morgan had occupied yesterday. With him were two men wearing dark golf shirts. All of them were wearing shades and looking way too serious to be tourists.

Mackenzie parked the car, but Morgan made no move to get out.

"What's the matter?"

"Him . . . the guy with the hat." Morgan pointed to him. "He was hassling me at the airport last week. He's really creepy. I really wouldn't want him to see me walk into the restaurant."

"The one with the flowered shirt and the bristly face?" Mackenzie asked, sounding somewhat alarmed.

"Yeah, Old Porcupine Butt. Why? Do you know him?"

Mac nodded. "Yeah, he's pretty well-known on the island. His name is Lorenzo. They call him 'the Chin.' He's originally from Colombia, but now he spends most of his time on Aruba. Unfortunately. Word is that he's connected to a cartel of drug dealers in South America. I've also heard stories that he works with the Mafia in America."

Morgan shivered. She'd been alone with this creep and then had almost run into him again at the beach. "Why don't they arrest him?"

"They have once or twice, but he always gets out. He's a middle guy, according to the rumors. The deal maker. They can never tie anything to him directly. He's just the slime who sets the table for something to happen. He collects a commission and stays in the clear."

Morgan thought about that for a moment, and then glanced sharply at her friend. "How do you know so much about him?"

Mac shrugged. "It's a small island. But I

know him personally because he was hitting on my mother for a while a couple of years ago."

"She's way too nice for a creep like him."

"I agree. It scared the crap out of me. But it was a perfect setup for him. Never mind that she's good-looking, but she also runs a business in the high-rent district of the island. Thank God she wouldn't have anything to do with him. She told me everything she'd heard about him so I'd know what was going on." Mackenzie planted her arms on the steering wheel and stared at the trio sitting around the table. "She's probably in the back fuming right now. He does this every now and then. Brings whoever he's setting up a deal for to the restaurant. He knows she won't kick him out."

"Why not?"

Mackenzie motioned toward the thugs by the cars. "If you don't treat Lorenzo with respect, there's a price to pay. She doesn't want to have the place burned down one night. And she also likes her face the way it is."

"He'd do that? Hurt her like that?"

"He's done worse," Mac said grimly.

"What a total creep! Who are the people with him?"

Mac shook her head. "I don't know them. Probably just in for the weekend to close some deal." She followed Morgan's gaze toward the cars.

"And them?"

"The younger guy with the two bruisers is even worse. Don't go anywhere near him. He likes to be called Tony, but I don't think that's his real name. The Chin says Tony is his nephew. I think he's lying, though. I think he's just a hired goon who watches the Chin's back and does his dirty work."

It was no different in Boston, Morgan figured, or anywhere else in the States. There were normal people that went about their lives, and then there were those few bad eggs. She just wanted to make sure that their paths never crossed.

"So what happens now?" she asked Mackenzie.

"Nothing, as far as I'm concerned. My mom won't come out of the kitchen until he leaves. The Chin does his business, then leaves a ridiculously large tip on the way out."

"I don't want him to see me. I'd just as soon be invisible around that guy."

"I don't blame you," Mackenzie said, starting the car again. "I'll pull up in the back. You can go through the kitchen door and hang out there with my mom. I'll come and get you when the coast is clear."

"What . . . the two of us can hide out while you go and face the big bad wolf?"

Mac gave her a wink. "Hey, his tip is going to pay for my spa treatment tomorrow. It'll be worth it."

They sat at either end of the sofa. Morgan's left foot was under Cy's butt. His hand absently massaged her calf. The containers of leftover Chinese food had been moved to the kitchen counter during the last commercial break. The movie they were watching was one that they'd both seen at least a half dozen times.

Even if it were the first time she was seeing it, Morgan would have still had a hard time focusing on the movie. Her gaze continued to drift to his profile. It still seemed impossible that he found her attractive. That he'd chosen her over Kate. She understood Mackenzie's feelings.

He reached over and turned off the light on the end table next to him. They'd closed the vertical blinds on the sliding glass door some time ago. The only light left on was the one in the kitchen, and the shadows stretched over them. He looked at her, and Morgan felt the tug low in her belly. He wanted her, and she wanted him. A commercial came on.

"I used to hate commercials." She inched toward him. "But they do have their pluses."

Taking his face in her hands, she placed soft kisses on his chin, his cheeks, his straight nose, before rubbing their lips softly together. She could read so much in his eyes. Desire, emotion. He threaded his fingers into her hair, drew her close, and deepened the kiss.

Morgan was the one who had told him they were moving too fast a day ago. But tonight, she was the instigator. As their mouths played a seductive dance, her hands moved under his shirt, running all over the hard muscles on his chest and stomach. He was amazing, beautiful, and she couldn't remember ever being as consumed by anything or anyone as she was by him.

The commercial ended. She slowly drew back on the sofa. He caught her ankle and put her foot on his lap.

"You're driving me crazy, Morgan," he whispered thickly, his eyes traveling down every inch of her.

She might as well have been naked the way his gaze scorched her skin. Her foot moved restlessly on his lap, and she bit her lip.

"You keep on like this, and all bets are off."

"You don't scare me," she whispered back.

"I was hoping you'd say that." His hand slid up the inside of her leg, sending shock waves up through her body . . . shock waves that immediately turned to panic at the sound of a key in the slider door. Cy immediately withdrew his hand and laid a pillow casually in his lap.

Morgan sat bolt upright and glanced at the clock. 9:00. A second later, Philip pushed through the blinds. He stopped short, obviously surprised to see them there sitting together.

"Hi," he said. "Watching something good?"

They both waved a greeting.

"*Billy Madison*," Morgan said. Her father looked totally exhausted. "Have you had dinner yet? There's plenty here."

"Sounds good. But I think I'll take a shower first."

Morgan didn't miss the look that he gave them as he went by. He obviously guessed what they'd been up to. *Well*, she thought, *if he brings it up, tonight would be a good time to explain a few things to him.*

"I'm gonna run," Cy told her after Philip disappeared into his bedroom.

"You don't have to go."

"I know." He brushed a kiss on her lips and smiled. "You're totally amazing. I'd love to keep you all to myself. But remember what we talked about this morning? About giving him a chance to be your father *and* your friend? By the looks of things, you're going to have to grab whatever time he has."

She understood.

"Plus, I think I need a shower, too. A long, cold one."

She smiled as Cy got up to leave. As he went out, she decided to leave all the windows and the slider open. The fresh air felt good, and the scent of flowers drifted in from the courtyard.

Morgan went to the kitchen to make sure the food was still hot. It wasn't, so she put what was left on a large dish and stuck it in the microwave. While she was setting out a plate and silverware for Philip, she saw him go back and forth between the bedroom and his office. He hadn't taken a shower yet.

"Did Cy go?" he asked.

She nodded, her mind going back to what she'd seen in his desk last night.

"By the way," she said, "I was wondering if I could use your computer to check my e-mail. Our PC at home died the week before I left Boston, and it feels like forever since I've been in touch with any of my friends."

She noticed the slight hesitation, but he recovered quickly. "Sure. You can bring it out here, if you want."

"No. I'd rather be sitting at your desk, actually. It'd be easier on my leg."

"In that case, let me boot it up for you."

She came around the counter. "I know how to do it."

"I have a security system that you have to get past. I'll do it."

Morgan followed him into his office. The black briefcase was back and sitting next to the desk. There was a green folder open that he quickly closed and tucked under one arm. He opened the laptop and switched it on.

She looked around the room, turned on a couple of lights, including the one on the desk. Everything looked so neat and clean and almost sterile, like the rest of the house. She thought about what Cy had mentioned to her this morning—about Philip's project, whatever it was. She wondered how he would celebrate when he was done. There was nothing exciting to come back to here, that's for sure. Absolutely nothing exciting . . . like his life.

Morgan looked at her father and the weariness she saw in him tugged at her heart. "Why don't you have a girlfriend?"

His blue gaze lifted off the screen and met hers. Surprise quickly turned to amusement, wrinkling the corners of his eyes. "A girlfriend?"

"Oh. Maybe you have one and just don't want to introduce me to her."

"No. No girlfriend at present."

"And why is that?"

"Wait a minute. This isn't the way this discussion is supposed to go. I'm supposed to be asking *you* these kinds of questions."

"Well, I'm your daughter. I think I have a right to know."

"Really?" He ran a hand over his face. "To be honest, this was the discussion that I really wanted to have with you. I want to know about your relationships."

"Mine is very simple, and you can pat yourself on the back for setting it up." She sat in one of the chairs. "Cy and I are going out. Girlfriend and boyfriend. Having a relationship, as you put it."

He sat back in his chair. "When did this start?"

"When I was two and he was five or six. I've been carrying a torch for him ever since."

He stared at her for a couple of seconds, gauging her seriousness. She smiled, and he seemed relieved. "I see. A long-term relationship. And how serious is this?"

Very, but she wasn't going to tell him that.

"Is there any problem with going out with him?" she asked instead, feeling a bit defensive.

"None whatsoever," he quickly replied. "I

guess I'd just be a little concerned that he's three years older than you. And he goes to college. How do I put this? I know you probably think it was the Dark Ages when I was in college, but my vague recollection is that college boys' . . . uh, expectations are somewhat different than those of high school boys."

"Well, I only had one boyfriend in high school, and he happened to have much . . . much greater expectations than Cy does." She almost laughed to see him grow immediately tense.

"What did he want?" he asked.

"Sex."

He cleared his throat. His face looked a little flushed. "What did you do?"

"I told him no."

"What happened?"

"He broke up with me the day before the junior prom."

"The miserable little . . ." He bit back what he was going to say. "Please tell me you didn't mope over such a loser. Tell me that you went to prom without him and had a fantastic time."

"That would have been a very happy

ending to a pathetic tale."

"You didn't go?"

"As a matter of fact, I did. My best friend, Becca, and her boyfriend convinced me to go with them. Other kids were going stag, so I did, too."

"Did you have a good time? Because that would have really shown him that you are not to be—"

Morgan held up a hand to stop him and shook her head sadly from side to side. "When I was getting ready to leave the house, I tripped over my gown, fell down a flight of stairs, and broke my leg. I spent the night of the prom in the emergency room."

"Alone?"

"Jean was with me." That night, Morgan had shed all the tears she was going to. The emotions caused by losing Jack and missing the prom and ruining the most expensive dress she'd ever worn all poured out in one good cry.

Of course, there were other reasons for the tears, reasons she couldn't explain to Jean. Her mother's marriage to Kabir marked the end of an era. Morgan felt she was losing the only parent she'd ever been able to rely on. She wouldn't be Jean's best friend anymore. Never again would she be at the center of her mother's attention.

Morgan had been totally drained, but she'd actually felt much better the next morning. The doctors had given her leg six weeks to heal. She'd given herself the same length of time to get over her problem with her mother's marriage and everything else that was changing in her life.

To Morgan's relief, the six weeks for the leg had been extended to eight. She doubted even that would be enough time to straighten out her problems with her father.

Philip stared at a spot just beyond her right shoulder for a long time. Finally, he spoke. "I'm sorry, Morgan. I wish I could have been there for you, too."

Shit. Morgan felt her armor slipping, the emotions rising through cracks in the crust of her defenses. She blinked a couple of times and tried to focus on the pattern of the throw rug.

"I have no problem with your relationship with Cy," he said, after a minute.

She looked up and nodded. She still

didn't trust her voice.

"This is ready for you," he said, motioning to the laptop. He got up from the chair and came around the desk. "I think I'll go and take that shower now."

Morgan sat and watched him leave the office. He seemed as shaken up as she was. She didn't know why, but his words had come as a surprise. It was a totally weird feeling, knowing that he'd wanted to be with her that night in the hospital. What he was saying was that he really wanted to be part of her life. The good days and the bad ones, too.

And she believed him.

The shower began to run in the master bathroom. Morgan came around the desk and tested the drawer that had been left open last night. It was locked. She checked another drawer. The entire desk was locked up.

Trust him. The words echoed in her head. She wanted to. She had to.

Morgan sat behind the desk and logged into her e-mail account and the world in Boston that she'd left behind a million years ago.

Chapter 18

They were directed toward two adjoining rooms in the Radisson hotel's health club. Morgan sent a nervous glance at her friend as the thin woman who was her masseuse waited for her to go inside first.

"You'll love it," Mac assured Morgan, giving her a big smile.

The room was small, maybe six by eight. The lights had been dimmed. Soft music played in the background. A high narrow table, padded and covered with layers of white sheets and towels, sat in the middle. There was a dish on top of a plug-in burner in a corner, filling the air with a pleasant scent that she couldn't identify. She also saw a number of bottles of oils and creams on the same table that held the burner.

Her name was Kyrenia. They'd been first introduced outside when Morgan and Mackenzie had arrived. She spoke English with an accent, and had a very pleasant smile.

"Okay. Everything off. Lie under the towel, facing up."

"Everything?" Morgan asked, growing increasingly uncomfortable.

Kyrenia nodded. "I wait outside."

There was no room for argument. The clock was ticking. Morgan stripped out of her sundress and underwear and threw them on the chair. Naturally, the hem of her dress caught one of the bottles on the table, and she nearly dove to catch it. Losing her balance, she bumped the table hard and a half dozen bottles fell over and started rolling toward the edge.

In seconds, she had a juggling act going. She caught two, but the rest fell to the floor. Thankfully, none of them broke.

Morgan was still putting the bottles back on the table when she heard a knock on the door.

"Five seconds," she pleaded, replacing the last bottle.

As she tried to get under the towel, her cast banged the leg of the table so hard it sounded like a gong. She was still struggling with the towel when Kyrenia walked back in.

Five seconds obviously meant five seconds.

The masseuse dimmed the lights a little more. The volume of the music went up slightly. She walked over to the corner where the oil and creams were. If she noticed it, she didn't say anything about Morgan's rearranging job.

"Relax, honey," the woman whispered, picking up one of the bottles.

Easier said than done. Morgan noticed that the door was very flimsy and there were no locks. What happened if someone decided to come in? She couldn't see what Kyrenia was doing, and that was nerve-racking, too. She felt too exposed.

Just as Morgan was getting ready to call the whole thing off, Kyrenia's hands appeared before her face, her palms over her nose.

"Breathe."

She followed the direction and took a deep breath. Whatever was on the masseuse's hands smelled wonderful. Morgan took another breath and then another. In all of thirty seconds, she was beginning to feel very relaxed. *Whatever that is*, she thought, *it can't be legal.*

Kyrenia went to work. There was no talking. Only the music and the scents and the feel of warm oil being massaged onto her face by competent hands. Morgan lost track of time. Her shoulders and arms were next and then she had to roll over and her back became the target of the masseuse's attentions.

By the time Kyrenia reached her legs, Morgan felt like a total ragdoll. Somewhere in the back of her brain, it suddenly sank in why so many people religiously got weekly massages: to relax.

Morgan wondered what would happen if she made an appointment for Philip. She wondered if he would go. Maybe she'd just run that by him first.

Outside of the room, Mackenzie and Morgan met for a minute before they went off to their next stop on the spa tour.

"I'm only getting a manicure," Morgan told her friend. "The pedicure will have to wait until this leg comes out of the cast."

"How many days left?"

"Six," she said with a sigh.

"Well, have fun with the manicure. I'll probably still be with the hairdresser when you finish. Come and see me there."

Morgan felt a lot less trepidation in getting

her nails done. It wasn't something she did regularly, but it wasn't a totally foreign experience. Plus, she didn't have to get naked for it. She recalled the last time she'd had her nails done. It was the week before the prom.

Well, here's to new beginnings, she thought.

Forty minutes later, she joined her friend in the salon. Mac was still under the hand of the stylist, and Morgan grinned at the face she made at her. Mac waved her closer.

"Watch what you say," she whispered as soon as Morgan was close enough to hear.

Morgan looked around and saw what Mac was referring to: the Lizards. Kate was getting wrapped in foils for highlights, and Ellie was getting her hair blow-dried. Liz and Beth were waiting in chairs.

She turned her back to them and watched what the stylist was doing to Mac.

"Can you believe it? She cut my hair even shorter!"

"You look beautiful," Morgan said in earnest, seeing for the first time what was done. Her hair *was* much shorter, accentuating Mac's curls. "This is Halle Berry style. It looks gorgeous on you. It'll be so much easier to pick out

the perfect dress, too. You should wear something that shows lots of cleavage."

"We'd better find a dress that comes
with it."

"Come on, you have plenty," Morgan said
positively.

"Sounds like the girl's speaking from first-
hand experience," one of the Lizards said,
drawing snickers from the other three.

Morgan turned around and took in the
amused looks on the four women's faces. "So
the Lizards *do* come in out of the sun."

"You should be careful," Kate said from
under her tent. "M&M's are known to *melt* in
the sun."

So, they were the M&M's now? Well, the
gloves were off, then, and Morgan started to
respond.

Kate had to ruin it, though, by suddenly
smiling pleasantly at her. "We're just teasing
you a little. You two started the name-calling,
you know."

"You're right," Morgan said, pasting a fake
smile on her face. "And what's a little teasing
between friends?"

"Exactly." Kate looked at her nails. "By the

way, where you able to pass on my message to Cy?"

"Of course. Didn't he call you?" Morgan tried to sound shocked.

Kate lowered her chin, hiding the upper half of her face under the metal tent. "He probably did. We haven't been home much lately to check our messages."

Total denial, Morgan thought. *Enjoy it.*

"So, are you two coming to the party?"

Morgan met Mackenzie's gaze in the mirror. She gave her an encouraging wink. "We might poke our heads in. Can we bring our dates?"

"You mean each other?" Beth cracked.

All of them but Kate had a good laugh about that. Morgan figured she was either playing the part of the suffering saint, or she hadn't heard the joke because of all the radio stations she was picking up through the metal antennae on her head. Morgan bet it was the latter.

"Can we bring guests?" she repeated.

"Absolutely."

"Great."

Thankfully, the hairdresser was just finishing up with Mackenzie, and within fifteen minutes, the two friends were on the road to Oranjestad for lunch and dress shopping.

"So you're going to the party," Mac said happily.

"Not only am I going, Cy is coming as my date."

"That's fabulous," Mackenzie said with enthusiasm. "I knew you two would end up with each other."

There was no denying it. Not to Mac. She'd been so open with Morgan about her feelings for Nick.

"I'm crazy about Cy. But at the same time . . . I'm scared shitless."

"That's what love is all about." Mac smiled, her eyes flitting from the road to Morgan and back again.

"I don't think this is about love. I think this is more about being a Callahan. I mean . . ." She paused and gathered her thoughts. "I mean, I come from a broken marriage . . . and, in a way, I know I'm to blame."

"That's absurd. All kids think the divorce is their fault, but it never really is."

"Seriously," Morgan continued. "I don't think they were ready to be parents when they had me. When I was little, they insisted on me calling them by their first names."

"That's why you call your father 'Philip'?"

Morgan nodded. "It wasn't until this past year, when Jean started getting serious with Kabir, that she noticed maybe being called a mother would give her more authority over me. So then it was 'Mom.' I mean, come on!" She shook her head in frustration. "They're a total mess. I'm a total mess."

"No, you're not," Mackenzie scolded her. "Lord, I wish I had a tape recorder, so you could hear yourself talk. This is just jitters, girl. You sound exactly the way I sounded a couple of days ago."

Morgan glanced at her friend. "You're not like that anymore?"

She shook her head from side to side. "Definitely not. I'm a new woman, and I'm determined to let all that pampering do some good."

"Okay," Morgan said. "Then I'm with you."

They both laughed.

"By the way," Mac said. "I like our new nickname."

"M&M." She didn't mind it, either.

"Maybe we should come up with our own music label." Mac made a face. "I think the name's been taken, though."

"A couple of times, at least. But it's probably for the best. I . . ." Morgan was going to say that most of the singing she'd done had been in the shower, but the words withered on her tongue. She stared at some men standing near a black limo on the street they were passing.

"Stop," she said as they passed the corner. "Stop here."

Mackenzie veered to the right, cutting another car off and almost causing an accident. She pulled onto the gravel shoulder of the road and slammed on the brakes.

"What's wrong?"

"I saw Philip." Morgan pushed the door open and got out. She didn't bother with the crutches and started hurrying as fast as her leg would allow her to go. It seemed to take forever, but within a minute she was standing at the corner, peering around the edge of a building.

The street was empty. The car was gone.

She'd seen her father. She was absolutely

certain it was him. Worse, he was talking to one of the men who'd been sitting with Lorenzo yesterday at the restaurant. The two bodyguards were there, too. One of them was holding the door of the limo, while Philip got in with them.

A couple of seconds later, Mackenzie came roaring up in reverse against the oncoming traffic. She slammed on the brakes at the corner. She rolled down the window.

"Morgan, what's going on?"

Her father was getting into a car with drug dealers. Great. How do you say that to your friend?

"I wish I knew."

Chapter 19

It was late in the afternoon when the two girls got back to Morgan's house. They'd decided to get Mac ready at the villa for her date, since she was planning to come back after the dinner cruise and stay the night.

The dress they'd chosen for her was gorgeous. An aqua pastel paisley print in a soft, flowing material. The knee-length skirt was flattering and perfect on her. The neckline was a crossover V, but the back plunged, ending in a deep slit. The dress was hot, to say the least.

Morgan thought there was no need to wear anything over it. It wasn't like it would be cold on the water. Aruba had to have the most perfect weather anywhere. Besides, Mackenzie looked absolutely beautiful and incredibly sexy in the dress. Mac wasn't convinced, though. Shy about all the skin showing, she'd insisted on picking up a hand-crocheted shawl of an almost identical color from her mother's house.

As Mac draped it around her shoulders,

Morgan kept her comments to herself about Mackenzie still looking sizzling hot for fear of her friend deciding against the dress altogether.

"I don't like your shoes with them," Morgan objected, pointing to the black sandals Mac had on. They wore the same size shoes. She offered a pair of white leather ankle-strap slides. "Why don't you try these?"

Mac slipped her feet in and looked at herself in the mirror. "You're right. That looks much better."

Morgan had helped her put on a little mascara and lip gloss before donning the dress. Mac had such perfect bronze skin that anything more and Morgan thought it would take away from her natural beauty.

"And what do you think of this necklace with the dress?" Morgan moved behind her and held a double-drop necklace against Mac's throat.

"It's beautiful," Mac whispered. "But I can't take it. I'd be too afraid to lose it."

"You won't lose it. And if you do, it's no big deal," Morgan assured her. "I made it myself."

"No way."

Morgan nodded, showing her how the cord

was made of natural-colored leather and the drops were dark blue stones she'd found at a crafts fair.

"I'll be really careful."

"I'm not worried," Morgan said, clipping the necklace around her neck.

They both heard the sound of Nick's car pulling into the driveway. Mackenzie turned to Morgan one last time, the edge of panic in her face.

"Oh, my God. That's him. How do I look?"

"You look awesome." Morgan started pushing Mac toward the door. "Now, don't forget. No laughing, no drinking, no kissing, no touching . . . and definitely, no having a good time."

"Yes, Mom." Mac paused by the door. "What time Cy is getting home tonight?"

"He was going sailing after work. A couple of runs, and he thought he should be home before it got dark."

"I can't wait till you're out of this cast. I really think you'll love the sport."

"I'm definitely going to try to learn it. We'll go from there," Morgan said, following Mac out through the front door.

Nick was waiting next to his car. All cleaned up, he looked pretty hot, too. He only had eyes for Mackenzie, though, as Morgan wished both of them a great time.

As Nick went around to get in the driver's side, Morgan admired her friend's taste. Nick was quiet, not a ladies' man who played the field. More the studious type. In Morgan's mind, this was another mark in his favor. Actually, the two seemed to be perfect for each other.

She leaned against Mackenzie's car, watching Nick back out and start down the road. She waved and started to turn toward the villa.

She stopped and looked back down the road. A white car was parked about four or five houses up. She'd lived here long enough to know that unless there was a party, no one left their cars along that stretch of the road. She didn't think anyone was living in the house where the car was parked.

The setting sun cast a glare on the windshield, but she could see there were two people sitting inside. She couldn't make out anything else.

Morgan walked back into the villa. After

locking the door, she went to a window and peered out at the road. The white car had moved. It was now parked closer to the house.

She stood there, watching it, prickles of fear running down her back.

"What's this all about?" she muttered.

It could have been five minutes or fifteen — she lost track of time — but finally the passenger door of the car opened. A tall man in a flowered shirt and sunglasses stepped out. He had a crew cut and looked to be balding in front. He stood there for a couple of minutes, leaning against the car and apparently talking to the driver. Morgan saw him look around and then look back at the villa.

They had seen her come back inside alone. Morgan shuddered at the thought of one of them knocking on the door. She wouldn't answer it. They could try to break in, though.

Her mind wouldn't slow down enough to think of what they might want. She just figured it had to be bad.

Looking around the villa, she tried to remember if there were any other doors or windows that might have been left unlocked. The air-conditioning was blasting, so she doubted it.

She wasn't going to take any chances, though, flimsy locks or not. As quickly as she could, she went around the house, making sure every door and window was locked.

Her broken leg was suddenly a huge liability. Morgan wanted the cast off. Now.

As she closed the last shade, it occurred to her that they'd probably seen her closing them. It didn't matter, she thought, they were closed now and she wasn't answering the door.

She grabbed her phone and dialed Cy's number at work. A woman answered and told her he'd already left for the day. Morgan introduced herself and asked for her father next.

"I haven't seen Mr. Callahan since he left this morning."

"When was that?" she asked.

"Around eleven," the woman explained. "I don't believe he's coming back today, either."

Morgan thanked the woman and hung up. Cy didn't like to carry a cell phone. He said he didn't need it on Aruba, and there weren't enough people that he knew on the island that he'd want getting hold of him.

But he and Philip insisted that Morgan carry hers around. *Damn it*, she thought.

Philip. He carried a phone. He'd given her the number. Morgan picked up her phone again and speed-dialed him. She got his voice mail.

"Unbelievable." Not much point in leaving a message, she decided, since she'd be dead.

Emergency numbers. She didn't know what they were in Aruba. There was a fat copy of Aruba phone book in the kitchen. She pulled it out now and checked the numbers for police and fire.

Phone in hand, Morgan walked toward the front door again and peered out.

Both men were now out of the car. The driver was small and compactly built, like a Mini Cooper. If anything, though, the look on his face made him just as intimidating as his partner. The two men looked up and down the road and then started toward the villa.

Her muscles seemed to freeze, and Morgan stood where she was, watching them come.

Chapter 20

Cy slammed on the brakes and stared at the villa.

A fire engine and a police car blocked the road right in front of the Callahan place. Sandwiched against the fence was Mackenzie's ancient car.

"Morgan," he whispered. Throwing the car into park, he jumped out.

Immediately, he heard sound of men talking and laughing, and the voices were definitely coming from the courtyard.

The hoses on the fire engine were still in place. Neither emergency vehicle had its lights on. There was no group of spectators watching the action. Most important, there was no ambulance. They'd just decided to use the road as a parking area, apparently. He strode toward the villa.

He stopped dead when he heard Morgan's voice over the rest.

"Tuma aki, pa fabor."

He understood enough of the words in her broken Papiamento to figure she was asking someone to take something. Cy stood there for a couple of seconds, letting his heart climb back into his chest, and then walked toward what was beginning to sound like a party.

The guests started to leave, though, before he made it to the gate.

A firefighter went by with a handful of cookies. He'd shed his gear and was wearing a T-shirt and khaki work pants.

"Bonochi," the fireman said with a mouthful, as he passed. "She's nice, that girl."

"Bonochi," Cy said, wishing him a good evening in return. He stared after the man for a second and then stopped to talk to a young police officer who came through the gate next. *"Ta kiko a pasa?"*

Cy quickly realized his mistake in asking in Papiamento, as the officer rattled off an explanation in his native tongue, totally leaving him in the dust.

"What happened?" Cy asked the question again in English.

This time, there was no immediate answer, only a rather wary look. "What's your name?"

"Cyrus Reed."

"Do you live here?"

"Yes, in the guesthouse. Right there." Cy pointed.

"Is she your girlfriend?"

"Yes," Cy said firmly.

"Too bad. She's very nice."

There seemed to be a consensus that Morgan was nice. "I know."

"You're being good to her?"

"Absolutely," he stressed, feeling himself getting a little suspicious of the man's interest in Morgan. "What happened in there?"

"The young lady called in about a fire. The truck comes out, and we get the call to come out, too. My partner and I happened to be at the Fisherman's Huts, so it was no problem."

"I'm glad," Cy replied. "Where was the fire?"

"She said she saw sparks coming from one of the plugs in the kitchen." The officer said something in Papiamento to two firefighters who came out the gate. They both looked at Cy and said something he didn't understand.

He looked questioningly at the officer. "We all like her. You *are* being nice to her?"

"I told you I am," he said defensively.

It seemed that the last members of the fire-fighting crew were leaving the courtyard. Cy figured he'd find out the rest of what happened from Morgan herself.

"We didn't find anything of any fire," the young officer said with a smile. "But she's very nice."

Cy thanked him, but before he could get to Morgan, the firefighters were calling him back to move his car. Once the emergency vehicles got past him, he parked next to Mac's car and got out. Morgan was waiting for him.

"I thought I saw you out front," she said, coming around the car. She came right into his arms and held him.

"Are you okay?" he asked.

Her head bumped his chin when she nodded, but Cy didn't believe her.

"What's wrong?" he asked.

She pulled away and looked up and down the street. The sun was just dropping into the Carribbean and a light breeze was cooling the air. She was obviously looking for something, but Cy had no idea what it was.

"What's going on?"

She nodded down the road. "There were a

couple of men in a white car watching the villa," she said finally.

"When?"

"I noticed them when Nick came over to pick up Mackenzie for their date."

Morgan had told him before that Mac was staying at the villa overnight.

"How do you know they were watching this house?"

"I had a pretty good idea when they got out of the car and started walking toward the villa."

"What happened then?"

"I didn't want to call the police and say, 'Hey, I'm scared. Someone is crossing the street.' So I called the fire company and told them the first thing that came into my head."

Cy walked up to the edge of the road and looked both ways, but there were no other cars. He came back to her.

"I'm sorry, but I was really scared, and there was no one else I could call. I didn't know what to do."

"I think you did great." He kissed her forehead and wrapped an arm around her shoulder, leading her into the courtyard. "I think that was genius."

"I felt so stupid, though. There was no knock on the door, and nobody tried to break in before the firefighters showed up. I was probably scared for nothing."

"I don't think so. I think you did the right thing," Cy said, helping her gather up napkins and plastic cups left on the table in the yard. "Most of the houses in this neighborhood are owned by Americans. I'd say two-thirds of them sit empty this time of the year. I don't think they have too much trouble with break-ins in Aruba, but you never know. You always have to go with your instinct."

He followed her as she went inside the villa. A cookie sheet and mixing bowls had been piled into the sink. The smell of home-baked chocolate chip cookies permeated the air.

"You were baking cookies?"

She nodded. "Sorry. They ate all of them."

"They?"

"The firefighters and the two police officers." She started stacking the bowls in the dish-washer. "I felt so guilty. I mean, I knew they wouldn't be finding anything. So I figured the least I could do was bake them some cookies.

I think they liked them. They ate the entire three dozen."

"Every single one of them told me how wonderful you are."

A beautiful smile broke across her lips. "They were trying to teach me Papiamento. The younger of the two police officers asked me a couple of questions that I didn't understand. By the way the rest of them laughed, though, I think he was asking me out on a date."

"What did you tell him?" Cy asked, coming around the counter.

"I said I have a boyfriend," she replied, turning to him.

"Right answer." He took her into his arms and softly kissed her lips. The way she leaned into him drove him crazy, made him want to do more. A lot more. Her mouth was soft, her tongue playful, dancing with his until he groaned in frustration. He pulled back, his forehead resting on hers.

"I'm glad that was the right answer," she said.

"They all told me that I had to be nice to you. Were you complaining to them?"

She took hold of the front of his T-shirt and

stepped back, taking him with her until she was leaning against the counter and he was pressed up against her. He was going to have to be locked up in a nuthouse if she didn't stop doing this to him.

"I guess I managed to mix up Spanish and English and Papiamento. One of them asked how I'd broken my leg, but I didn't understand him at first and totally thought he was asking something else. So I said, 'My boyfriend.' They stopped smiling right then, and I knew I hadn't answered the question correctly. I tried to explain, but I guess I didn't do a very good job."

"I was lucky I didn't get arrested out there."

"I wouldn't have let them," she said, pulling him closer and pressing kisses against his neck. "I would have protected you."

Cy planted his hands on either side of her on the counter, trying to control the rush going through him.

"Now that we've started talking about protection. You need to protect me from your father, too."

Morgan immediately looked up. "Why? What did he tell you?"

"I'm just kidding. It was no big deal."

"What? Tell me."

"Philip had 'the talk' with me first thing this morning at work."

"About what?"

"About us. You and me."

"You've got to be kidding me." Anger reddened her cheeks. "I don't see him for three years, and he thinks he has the right to meddle in my personal life *now*?"

"He does have the right. He's your father," he said gently. "But before you get too mad at him, you should hear me out."

It took a moment before her temper cooled down enough for her to look up at him. "Okay, what did he tell you?"

"To be nice to you. To take care of you. To treat you the way you deserve to be treated. Not to break your heart. To act responsibly . . . for both of us."

"Oh." She gazed into his eyes. "Are those things a hardship?"

"Not at all." He shook his head, teasing her lips with his mouth. "He did tell me, though, that he would break my leg if I had sex with you."

"He didn't say that."

Cy nodded.

"What did you say to that?"

"I told him I *would* have sex with you, but only when *you* were ready, and that he could be assured that I would act responsibly, take all the precautions."

A pretty blush had colored her cheeks. "And what did he say to that?"

"He told me to feel free to preorder my own crutches."

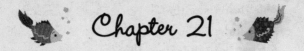

Chapter 21

If heaven came with white sand, clear skies, and water made up of so many shades of blue that a person could lose count, then the beach at Boca Grandi on the windward side of Aruba had to be that celestial paradise. Morgan leaned back on her elbows and felt the sun warming her skin.

"Don't burn," she reminded herself, reaching for the lotion again.

Two weeks ago, Morgan never would have admitted to anyone that she would willingly lie on a beach, still in a cast, wearing only a bathing suit top and some cutoff jean shorts. But here she was. And enjoying it, too.

Morgan looked at a tree on a low rise near the shore. Mac had pointed it out, telling her it was a divi-divi tree, the symbol of Aruba. It had the strangest shape for a tree, its trunk and branches brown and twisted like an ancient hand and holding a puff of greenery in its palm.

She sat up and shielded her eyes against the sun as she looked out at her friends racing across the water. The surf was high and powerful, and the spray often reached her, even where she was lying on her blanket far from the edge of the water. Cy had told her they were trying to get ready for Aruba's Hi-Winds Amateur World Challenge, a competition that would take place at the end of June. It was one of the most popular windsurfing competitions in the Caribbean, and the race attracted competitors from more than thirty countries.

Cy, Mac, and Nick were out in heavy swells far beyond the rollers crashing into the shore. As she watched, Morgan saw them all disappear into a trough. She frowned, thinking for the twentieth time that they must have been swallowed up by the sea, only to see Mac come flying up the far slope of the wave and sail straight up into the air. She flexed her legs expertly and dropped down smoothly into the next trough.

Cy was the next to appear, and that wasn't good enough for him, obviously. As the fins of his board cleared the top of the wave, Morgan watched him lean back, forcing his board into a backward somersault. She held her breath as he tumbled toward the water, and only let it out when he completed the flip and hit the water smoothly and in control. Nick followed, flying off the top of the wave, and he, too, quickly disappeared behind the other two into the next trough. They were amazing to watch.

It had been an educational experience hearing them talk this morning. Chop and reef passes. Jibes and broad reaches. Boardmakers named Geert. Sails named Pryde. Boards of carbon and kevlar. Bump and jump. Sheesh.

It was actually fun, though, to see how into it they were. She didn't really have a clue what they were talking about most of the time, but she did understand it when they said things like "scary fast."

My God, she thought. She was looking at scary fast now.

The three had come out into an area of slightly flatter water, and they were skipping across the surface like three triangular disks hurled from a slingshot.

Morgan lay back on the blanket again and pulled the baseball cap over her face. Except for the sound of the sea and the wind, it was quiet out here. Few tourists came to Boca Grandi, it seemed, preferring the calmer waters on the west coast of the island.

Last night, Cy had taken Morgan out to eat at an Italian restaurant overlooking those calm waters. The chairs and tables had actually been set on the beach with torches burning around the edges of the place. Morgan had loved the food, the atmosphere . . . and especially the company.

They hadn't talked again about her father's conversation with Cy about sex, but the thought wouldn't leave Morgan's mind. Cy's words about waiting for her to be ready continued to dance in her head. She wondered how long he would wait.

How long would she want him to?

Life was not as simple as deciding on something and going through with it. At least, not Morgan's life. She couldn't be happy. Here she was in paradise with a hot and attentive guy, and she was killing herself worrying about what would come after. When summer was over. She'd be in Boston. He'd be in D.C. Her parents had failed at their long-distance relationship.

Never mind the distance. Could they keep a relationship going that long? And would he want to?

Morgan realized she was giving herself a headache. Cy was thinking of today, tomorrow, this weekend . . . and she was already planning their retirement. She wished she could be more like Mackenzie. Her friend told her she and Nick had had a great time last night. But Mac wasn't picking out wedding dresses. She was only planning as far ahead as this morning's sailing. She was living in the moment and enjoying Nick's company *now*.

Morgan tore her cap off and sat up. She wondered if she were even capable of having a relationship. She shook her head. What a piece of work.

Looking out at the water, she saw that two other people had joined Cy, Mac, and Nick. Three more people were dragging equipment down onto the beach.

"Five more days," Morgan murmured. Five days and she'd be trying everything. Swimming, scuba diving, windsurfing, snorkeling, horseback riding. Name it, and she'd be up for it. She was *ready*.

She looked to the south, wondering if she dared to hazard a walk along the sandy beach. The tops of only a few houses could be seen in the distance, and the pretty Alto Vista Chapel was visible slightly inland, high on a hill. She looked north toward the lighthouse. There was nothing but sand and sea and rock in that direction.

Except for the two men sitting in the shade of a divi-divi tree just above the beach.

Morgan stared at the white car parked behind them.

A hundred yards offshore, Cy caught sight of Morgan pushing to her feet. He was thinking about taking the board for another run, but he decided against it. Instead, he jibed and headed straight for the shore.

She'd been sitting there for a couple of hours, and the sun was getting pretty high in the sky. For the last two runs, he'd begun to worry about her sizzling to a crisp. He'd brought a sun umbrella for her to the beach, but she'd refused to let him open it, telling him she'd take care of it. *She must be ready to get out of the sun*, he thought.

To his surprise, though, he saw she wasn't heading back to the car. She was walking north, in the direction of the lighthouse. The sand on the beach was soft, and as he got close to the shallows, he could see it was hard going for her with the crutches.

Guilt hit him like a wave. She was probably bored. As well as burnt. He called her as he hopped off the board, but he doubted she heard him.

By the time he came out of the water, he realized she wasn't following the beach, but climbing a low, stony embankment beyond the beach. By a grove of trees beyond it, he saw a white car. Two men were standing on either side of the car, the doors open, engaged in an animated conversation. He remembered what she'd told him last night. She'd seen two guys in a white car.

Cy ditched his board in the sand and took off after her. She'd made it a surprisingly good distance, despite the crutches. The stony incline she was on now, though, worked in his favor, and he caught up to her when she was halfway up the hill.

"Where are you going?" he asked, reaching her.

She seemed relieved to see him. "That's them. The two from yesterday. The ones who were watching the house."

"What were you going to do?"

"I'm going to ask them what they want."

"Morgan," he took her arm, forcing her to stop. "If these two are the same guys, and if you were the one who they were watching, don't you think it'd be total lunacy to approach them alone?"

She nodded. "But I'm not alone. You're with me."

"Yeah, but I wasn't a minute ago. You could have waited for me," he said, more sharply than he intended. "Look around you. If you reached them, and they decided to stuff you in the trunk, who would have even heard you scream?"

"You're being a little overly dramatic."

"No, I'm not. I'm worried about you. You can't keep doing dangerous things."

"I really wasn't trying to," she said softly. "Hey, I figured, if I got close enough, I could at least read the license plate on their car."

"And what were you going to do with that? Call your good friends at the police department?"

She stared at him for a moment, the color rising in her face.

"I might have," she said stubbornly.

Frustrated, Cy ran a hand through his hair. Standing there in that little bikini top and the jean shorts that showed off a knockout body, she didn't even realize how beautiful she was. She didn't know that two strange men in a place as secluded as this might just get some sick ideas . . . even if they weren't the same men from before. They could easily grab her, even if they didn't know her from Adam. Or Eve. Or whatever.

She looked up the hill. "They're gone."

He could see the white car was working its way up the rough road over the hills separating Boca Grandi from the rest of the island.

"You don't have to sound so disappointed," he said.

"Well, I am," she said. "I don't particularly like the idea of being a victim, and somebody watching me from a distance makes me feel like one. So if taking a two-by-four or a crutch to their heads is the answer, then I'm ready to go that route."

Before he could argue, she wheeled around and headed toward the parked cars, leaving a small bruise on his shin from her crutch as she swung around.

He had a feeling she was heading toward Mackenzie's car.

What the heck was he getting into? Morgan was stubborn, temperamental, and accident prone. He didn't particularly like the idea of having to explain their relationship to her father . . . who also happened to be his boss.

Then again, she was smart, funny, passionate, and beautiful. And he was falling hard for her . . . in the capital *L* sense of the word.

That was the scariest thing of all.

Chapter 22

Even though it was Saturday, Morgan was surprised to find her father working in his office at the villa when she got home around noon.

"You got burnt," Philip observed when she appeared in the doorway.

She looked down at her arms. She was definitely darker, and she could feel the tightness of the skin on her arms, legs, back, and chest. Even her face felt tight, despite the layers of sunblock and the hat and sunglasses.

"Are you sure it's not a tan?" she asked hopefully.

He smiled and shook his head. "You're going to hurt a little tonight."

The phone in the office rang, and Philip picked it up on the first ring. She had the feeling he was expecting the call. She heard him greet whoever was on the line in Spanish.

He made a gesture to her to give him five minutes. She nodded and backed out of the room. He came around to close the office door, and Morgan noticed for the first time the large, silver-colored briefcase sitting next to the desk. She hadn't seen it before.

She hung around in the living room. Even with the office door closed, she could still hear a smattering of what Philip was saying.

"Tengo el dinero . . ."

Morgan's curiosity was piqued. He was telling someone that he had the money.

". . . entrega . . ."

Delivery. Morgan thought that's what it meant, anyway. She got closer, her ear practically touching the door.

". . . mañana."

Tomorrow. She totally missed the next couple of sentences. Her father spoke Spanish with the speed of a native. Morgan did understand the last command: *Llámame. Call me.*

She quickly stepped away from the door and went to the kitchen before her father came out.

"Everything okay?" she asked as casually as she could muster when he appeared at the counter.

"Yes. Fine," he said, but he still seemed preoccupied.

"Did you have lunch?"

He shook his head. "Did you?"

"No."

Morgan bit her lip and thought about what to say. She didn't want to lose him. She wanted to know what was going on. Most important, she wanted to know that he was okay. That he wasn't getting himself into deep trouble. *Money, delivery, tomorrow.* The words didn't exactly fill her with confidence, and that made her angry. He was going to ruin it. Again. He was going to destroy this last chance they had.

"I can make us some grilled cheese, or a tuna sandwich."

"Either one. Your pick."

She caught him glancing at his office door.

"How about if you sit here and keep me company?" Morgan knew she was pressing her luck, but what the heck? "So who was on the phone?"

"Someone from work." He took her suggestion and sat on one of the high stools by the counter.

"By the way, were you in town yesterday?" When she glanced up, he averted his eyes.

"I might have been. Why? What time?"

"Around noon. I thought I saw you get into a car with—"

"It wasn't me," he said abruptly. He looked out the glass door at the guesthouse. "Where's Cy today?"

"I could have sworn it was you."

"No, it couldn't have been. Is he coming home for lunch?"

He was determined to change the topic.

"No, he was windsurfing this morning," Morgan answered, disappointed. "And they have some races this afternoon. They're trying to get ready for a competition in a couple of weeks."

"How did you get home?"

"My friend Mac, the girl who stayed over last night."

He nodded, his mind obviously cranking along. It was, apparently, on something else. Even with Mac's car in the driveway, it was clear to Morgan that he hadn't paid any attention to the note she'd left him, telling him exactly what was going on. She decided to make tuna sandwiches.

"Is everything okay between you and Cy?"

"Pretty okay . . . or at least I think it is,

despite all the Callahan foul-ups." Morgan took a loaf of bread and a can of tuna and put it on the counter.

"What do you mean by that?"

"I mean that there must be something genetically wrong with us," Morgan said. She needed to vent a little, and this was as good an opportunity as any. "I sometimes wonder if we're even capable of being happy. We go out of our way to do stupid things to mess up our lives and our relationships with other people . . . and with each other."

"You're exaggerating."

"I wish I were." She took the mayo out of the fridge and set it down on the counter with a bang. "I mean, look at the track record our family has. You and Jean are divorced. My two aunts, who happen to be your sisters, are on their second and third marriages. And when I left, it sounded like Aunt Bobbi's number three was looking a little rocky. The rest of Callahan relatives are incapable of even keeping in contact with other aunts and uncles and cousins."

"Bobbi and Dave are having marital problems?"

"It doesn't matter!" she almost shouted. "The

problem is we can't communicate. We keep everything in. We can't express our feelings. We hold grudges. And God forbid, if someone gets too close, or if there is the slightest possibility that a relationship is going to work out, then we just have to do something stupid to mess it up."

"You're doing okay in the communication department."

"But you're not."

He was doing exactly what she was talking about. Whatever deal it was that Philip had gotten himself involved in was just another attempt to push her away. Prison bars could work pretty well to create distance.

"Are you upset because of my talk with Cy yesterday morning?"

"No." His question gave Morgan's thunder a boost in a new direction. "But since you bring it up, do you really think that was necessary?"

"Yes, I do," he answered firmly.

"Why? Because you don't trust me?"

"Morgan—"

"Or is it that you think I have no values? That I wasn't brought up knowing how to make good choices?"

"I do trust you," he said passionately. "And I believe Jean has done an outstanding job of raising you. I just don't think having a relationship with a young man is the best—"

"Don't even go there." She shook her head. "But look what we've come back to. Relationships. Let's talk about *ours*."

"Okay. We've never had the opportunity to talk about—"

"Exactly. You can find the opportunity to talk tough with Cy, but you've never taken a minute to pull your own daughter aside and have the same talk with her."

"I did talk with you, Morgan." Philip crossed his arms over his chest. "But Cy is a young man. My guess is he's gone down this route before. Because he's older, he has to take more responsibility. My intention was for him to be aware of it."

"Your intentions, fatherly or otherwise, happen to be a little misdirected here. Before you try to play that authority game, or even pretend that level of concern, don't you think you should have some kind of rapport with your daughter? Don't you think she needs to know that your meddling is not because of your faulty Callahan genes, but it's because you're concerned as a father?"

He cleared his throat before he spoke. "I thought I'd done that."

Morgan swallowed hard, feeling her emotions blowing up like a volleyball in her chest.

"Maybe you've started," she said. "But to be honest, that's probably my biggest headache right now."

"What do you mean?"

She pushed the jar of mayo and the can of tuna away and leaned on her elbows on the counter, facing him.

"When I knew I was coming here for the summer, my only expectation was to be stuck in the house and have a horrible time. But things haven't gone as I expected. I've discovered in Cy a person that I can care about deeply. I've found a friend in Mackenzie. I've got a job. I'm loving the island. But do you know what's been the biggest surprise of all?"

He shook his head.

"I've started liking my father."

He reached across the counter and took her hand. "Morgan . . ."

"Don't." She shook her head and withdrew

her hand. "I don't want to like you because you're doing it again. You're making me get used to you. Making me want to accept you as my father. Then you'll just take it away again."

"That's not so, Morgan."

"But it is," she stressed. "You've done this to me over and over again. You've lied. You've gone away and stayed away. And you're doing the same thing now."

"It's my job. I know I haven't been there for you when you—"

She waved him off. "Is it your job to have five passports under different names? Is it part of your profession to hang out with dangerous drug dealers?"

He stared at her, a mask of hardness darkening his face.

"I need to know," Morgan asked in a softer voice. "Please tell me that nothing horrible is going to come out of what you're doing."

"Nothing horrible will happen," he said thickly, standing up.

"How do I know that?"

"You'll have to trust me, I guess."

Turning on his heel, he went across the

house to his office, and Morgan winced as the door closed. A moment later, she heard him talking on the phone. She wondered if he'd heard anything she'd said.

She wondered if it had *meant* anything to him at all.

Chapter 23

The place where Kate and her friends were holding the party turned out to be a gorgeous five-bedroom villa on the beach in Malmok. The wide-open layout at the center of the house was perfect for parties, with tiled floors and glass everywhere. The views were all Caribbean and gardens and pool.

The catered party had been set up around the pool, though, with tables piled high with finger foods and desserts and drinks. A small reggae band was playing on the far side of the pool. Torches had been set up everywhere, flickering and flaring in the light breeze.

"Now aren't you glad I talked you into coming, after all?" Mackenzie asked.

"No," Morgan said, stepping farther back into a bush as a group of laughing people tried to move past them.

Morgan's day had been miserable. She'd fought with Cy and argued with her father. She'd started to do the same thing with

Mackenzie when she showed up at the house in the afternoon. Mac wouldn't put up with it, though. She'd been determined that they were going to the party, even if she had to drag Morgan. And Morgan's excuses that she had a sunburn, that she was exhausted, and that she had a headache fell on deaf ears. Mac had simply bullied her into dressing up and coming to the party.

"Nick said he and Cy will try to get here by 9:00. They had an organizational meeting for the races tonight at the Fisherman's Huts."

"Do you know what time it is now?" Morgan asked.

"No, why?"

"I want to leave by 9:00."

Mac shot her a narrow glare. "You're being impossible, girl."

"I am not. Look at her," Morgan said through gritted teeth. Kate stood near the band, swaying to the music. She was dressed in a very short strapless white dress that hugged her curves like a glove. "She looks like one of the stars on *Baywatch*."

"Not a star," Mac corrected. "Only an extra. But since we're discussing looks, maybe you should go and stand in the bathroom. Go on, take a peek in the mirror at yourself. I'm telling you, you look hot."

"Yeah, that's because I'm burnt."

Mackenzie slapped her on the hand. "Fix that attitude. I just spotted two gorgeous men walking in."

Morgan glanced at the glass French doors of the villa and saw Cy and Nick. At the same time, she saw two of the Lizards pounce on them like five-year-olds on an ice-cream vendor. They obviously had their plan in place. Quite the reception committee, and Kate wasn't far behind. As she rounded the pool, her smile looked so bright Morgan figured people were probably being blinded in Venezuela.

"I'm going to greet Nick." Mac said. "Are you coming?"

"No," Morgan said in a small voice. "I think I'll just stay here and dig a hole I can crawl into."

As Kate approached, Cy grabbed the bottle of beer out of Nick's hand and held it up as if he were reading the label.

"Finally! I was expecting you this afternoon," Kate said, trying to loop her arms around his neck.

Cy continued to hold the bottle in that way, and then he took a sip out of it. In a split second, the whole thing became too awkward, even for Kate.

"Nice party," he said, looking at the crowd. "Is Morgan here?"

"Yes, she is," Mac answered, reaching them. Nick immediately put an arm around her and stole a kiss. Mac smiled and pointed, reluctantly taking her eyes off Nick. "She's by the garden. Oh, wait a minute. . . . There she is. She's walking by the pool."

Cy stepped away from Kate and looked that way.

"She's moping a bit, Cy. She had a real hard day. I'd say she needs a bit of TLC."

Her back was to him, and he let his gaze move appreciatively from the red curls tumbling onto her shoulders like a waterfall of fire to her beautiful bare back. A long skirt reached her shoes, hiding all but the toe of her cast. She turned to look at the band, and her gaze moved in his direction and caught his. He felt the sharp kick in his chest and started toward her.

"Not yet." Kate moved in front of him, pressing a hand to his chest. "There's something that I have to show you first. It's a surprise."

"Not now," he tried to go around her, but she blocked him again.

"It can't wait, Cy. It's inside."

"Then let me get Morgan, and you can show both of us your surprise."

"You can't spare five minutes for your girl?" She was pouting and hugging his arm.

"Look, Kate," he said sharply, peeling her off of him. "I only have one girl, and right now she's waiting for me to join her by the pool."

Cy didn't wait to see if his words sank in with Kate or not, for his attention was immediately drawn to a disaster being engineered before his very eyes.

Ellie was directing two of the waiters, who were holding one of the food-laden tables like a battering ram and backing toward the pool. Ellie was taking off a wrap, revealing a dress with a neckline that plunged to her navel, and continuing to motion the men backward. The waiters' eyes were fixed on her. Cy watched in horror as Ellie aimed the end of the table right at Morgan, who was now standing and facing the pool. It was like a slow-motion scene from a movie. Morgan was going to get knocked into the water.

"MORGAN!" he shouted.

She must have heard his voice over the music, for she turned just in time to see the table about to ram her off the edge of the pool. As she stepped aside, one of her crutches banged the leg of the table, and Cy saw it fold inward. The men whirled around, letting go of the table as they saw Morgan.

As one end of the table collapsed, the great shrimp slide began, and Cy watched all the food slip irrevocably toward the pool.

Morgan stared in stunned disbelief at the stuffed mushroom caps spreading onto the surface of the water.

A watermelon fruit bowl came next, but it went down like the *Titanic*. The swan centerpiece carved from ice made the leap into the pool and seemed to peck once at the mushroom caps, but then quickly went belly up. Cocktail shrimp dove in like shiny red lemmings.

A strong arm encircled her waist and lifted

her up, carrying her bodily away from the chaos.

"I won't have you taking all the credit for that," Cy whispered in her ear.

"It was amazing, wasn't it?" Morgan asked as he put her down at the edge of one of the gardens closer to the beach. "These crutches have been the best weapons."

"Yes, but this time they were used only in self-defense . . . and I'll take them now." He disarmed her and laid the crutches against a palm tree. "How about a walk on the beach until things get cleaned up in there?"

She looked down at her long skirt. "Walking in this *with* the crutches is a little bit difficult. Without them, I think a walk on the beach would be impossible."

The skirt was too tight. She shouldn't have listened to Mac. She should have just worn a pair of shorts or something.

"No problem."

Morgan squealed when she was lifted by Cy and shrieked when he tossed her over his shoulder.

"What are you doing?" she asked, dangling upside down.

"Going for a walk."

Sand was being crossed at a pretty good rate. "This is ridiculous! Cy, my brain is getting scrambled. Put me down."

"Not yet."

She tried to lift her head to see where they were going. He was almost at the water's edge. He turned left. But was it his left or her left? "I'm getting dizzy."

"I'll put you down in a minute."

"That might be too late," she complained. "I could end up with permanent brain damage."

In a few seconds, she found herself being gently placed on her feet next to two white lounge chairs. The water lapped the sand a couple of feet away. Morgan looked around, her head still spinning a little. She held on to Cy's shirt.

"I told you it would be too late. I can't see or think straight."

"Good," he whispered, pushing the hair out of her face. He took her chin in his hand and lowered his mouth to hers. "If you're not thinking straight, then I can take advantage of you."

He kissed her, and every inch of Morgan's

body came to life. He made her feel real, and his touch brushed away all the negative thoughts that had been buzzing in her brain. In his arms, she believed that there were no limits to what they could do.

"I'm sorry about this morning," she whispered as soon as his lips lifted from hers. "I'm really sorry about the way I behaved. About my carelessness in approaching those two guys. I know you were trying to be protective of me."

"I'm sorry about leaving you all alone on that beach."

She shook her head. "You were racing . . . or bumping and jumping . . . or whatever." She smiled. "I wanted to be there."

"Then I'm sorry I didn't come after you when you marched off."

"I was too upset to see clearly. I needed to cool off first."

"And did you?"

Morgan shook her head. "Actually, the day went from bad to worse. Until now."

He drew her into his arms again, and she rested her head against his chest. The music was playing once again at the party in the distance. Things appeared to have returned to normal.

"Do you think we should go back?"

"No," Cy replied softly. Sitting down on one of the chairs, he pulled her down with him. "I just want to stay here . . . with you."

Morgan nestled her back against his chest, and Cy's arms wrapped around her. They looked out in silence at the black water for a while.

"This is perfect," she finally murmured with a sigh.

A brightly lit cruise ship was moving slowly across the dark waters in the distance. The thought came to Morgan that there was nowhere else in the world that she'd rather be at this moment. Nowhere but in his arms. What she felt for him didn't frighten her anymore. She was ready to live her life.

"This is quite a dress," he said.

"You like it?"

"Way too much." He rubbed the fabric gently against her stomach. "We'll have to add it to the 'do not wear' list . . . unless you want your boyfriend's hands all over you."

Morgan turned her head and pressed a kiss

against his jaw. She wanted his hands all over her. She'd have to find another occasion to wear it.

"You got burnt today," he said, pushing her hair off her shoulder and pressing his lips to her fevered skin.

"Not burnt. Tanned."

"Is your tan painful?" She heard the smile in his voice.

"Very. But only in a couple of places."

"Where?"

"My arms, my face, my back, my chest, and my legs."

"Does it hurt here?" His thumb brushed over her breast.

She found herself arching her back, lifting herself into his hand. Sensations vibrated through her.

"No," she said softly. "It doesn't hurt there. Just everywhere else."

"Are you sure?"

She nodded. "I wasn't burned there. You can see for yourself."

Morgan couldn't believe that she'd said the words, but it was too late. His fingers deftly untied the string behind her neck. She almost brought a hand up to stop him, but the touch of his mouth on her neck numbed her.

The triangle of cloth dropped down. She felt the whisper of the breeze kiss her naked skin.

"You are so beautiful," he said hoarsely, sliding his fingers beneath her breasts.

Morgan thought she was going to die. She moved slightly in his arms, wanting more, not knowing how to ask. A couple's voices came from somewhere behind them. She immediately tensed, and Cy reluctantly pulled her shirt back up, tying it behind her neck.

"I have some great aloe cream for sunburn," he whispered in her ear. "It even smells good."

"I'm not burned," she corrected. "I'm tanned."

"Excuse me. I have some great lotion for tans that hurt."

"Really? Where?" she asked, leaning to the side to see his face.

"Back at the guesthouse."

She threaded her fingers through his hair and brought his mouth closer until she could taste him. "What are you saying?"

"I'm saying, if you come back there with

me tonight, I'll spread this amazing lotion all over you."

She swallowed. "You know that can lead to only one thing."

He nodded. "Me using crutches."

"You'd do that for me?"

He shook his head. "I'd go into a full body cast for you."

She sat up more and turned around until she could look into his face.

"I'd turn that whole party upside down for you," she replied. "I'd push every one of those partiers in the pool . . . starting with the lovely hostesses."

"For me?" Cy asked softly.

"For you."

"I love you, Morgan."

She froze, staring into his eyes, the breath caught in her chest.

"I've never felt what I feel for you with anyone else in my life," he said, cupping her face and bringing it closer to his. "I've never wanted anyone else as much as I want you. I know this kind of talk makes you ready to run, but that's okay. I just wanted you to know how I feel. As far as everything else, I'll wait for as long as you—"

Morgan put a finger to his lips, silencing him. "I love you back, Cy. There, I said it. And look, no thunderbolt appearing out of the sky to strike me. And no earthquake. I said it out loud and nothing horrible is happening."

No sooner had the words left her lips than she was aware of two figures standing not five feet from their chairs.

Lorenzo's nephew Tony and one of the gorillas that she'd seen at the restaurant moved toward the chair.

Tony was holding a gun in his hand.

Chapter 24

The midnight hour had come and gone some time ago, and the crowd at the party was starting to thin out a little. The hard-core were still here, though, and they were having no problem making up for the others in the dancing and drinking department.

Mackenzie watched Kate down another tequila and slither into the arms of Hans Something-or-Other, a young Dutch grad student who was standing by the dancing area and trying to look cool. Mac had gotten the scoop earlier. The guy was vacationing at one of the high-rise hotels. One of the Lizards—Beth, she thought it was—had met him this morning and invited him to the party. Of course, after Cy disappeared, Kate went on the hunt, and Hans was the next best thing. Aside from Nick, of course, but he was taken.

Mackenzie hurried toward the beach in search of her guy, only to find him walking back. She met him by the end of the gardens.

"Did you see them?"

"No," he replied. He pointed to one of the palm trees. "But they've left Morgan's crutches right here."

"What are they doing here?"

"Got me. But at least it could mean they're still around."

Mac looked back toward the house. "I need to be getting home. Morgan knew that I wanted to get out of here by midnight."

"Cy said the same thing to me. He didn't want to stay here that late, even." Nick rubbed her arm. "You and I both drove. I think you should go. I'll hang here and look around some more for them."

"Maybe I'll swing by the villa and give a quick knock at Cy's door. Morgan wasn't feeling too well tonight. I don't know why they would have, but maybe they hitched a ride with someone else and went home."

They both cast a doubtful look at the crutches.

"I'll keep looking here," he said.

Nick walked Mackenzie to her car. She'd parked a good two hundred yards down the road. As they walked, they passed a white car with the windows rolled down. Two men were sitting inside, listening to the radio. The night was too dark to see their faces. In the back of her mind, though, Mac remembered Morgan telling her about the two men that she felt were following her around. In a white car.

Mac looked back toward the car that they'd just passed.

"Everything okay?" Nick asked.

"Who were those guys?"

"I don't know. Maybe cops. They seem to be keeping an eye on things." He shrugged. "They don't seem to be a problem."

She hoped he was right.

Ten cars past the white one, things were not so serene. A guy and a girl were going at it in the back seat of an SUV. There was a lot of giggling and groaning and at the exact moment they were walking by, a woman's butt actually pressed against the side window for a few seconds.

"No problem there, either," Nick quipped, making her smile.

She stole a glance at him. Last night, after the dinner cruise, they'd had a few moments clinging to each other in the parking lot.

"You don't think anyone went by your car last night, do you?"

"Probably everyone leaving the boat did," he said lightly, putting an arm around her shoulder and bringing her close. "But compared to this production, I'd say our show was only rated G."

"Now, wait a minute," she said, reaching her car. "I had a little difficulty getting my dress to fit right, after that encounter."

He pressed his body against hers, trapping Mac against the car. "Well, I don't think my khakis have fit right since."

She looped her arms around his neck and brought his mouth down to hers. As she kissed him thoroughly, his hands were all over her body. Finally, she pulled back, trying to catch her breath.

His voice was a husky growl. "Do you want to come back to my place?"

Mac wanted to. She wanted to go with him. But she shook her head. "Not tonight. I'm already late getting back. And, to tell the truth, I have this real uncomfortable feeling about where Morgan and Cy might be. So will you . . . will you give me a rain check?"

"On the driest island in the Caribbean?" He kissed her lips. "You know I will."

"Thanks, Nick."

"I'll look some more around here," he said, straightening up. "We'll find them."

The office phone rang. Philip glanced at his watch first. It was ten after one. Still no sign of Morgan. He answered the phone on the third ring. There was no greeting at the other end.

"Alto Vista Chapel," the voice said.

"Why there?" Philip asked. The place was too open.

"I don't know," Lorenzo answered gruffly. "I only follow directions."

"What time?"

"There's a church service at 11:00. The delivery will be made during Mass."

Things were going from bad to worse. A public place that would be filled with tourists, as well as native Arubans.

"Can we make a change of location?"

"No," he answered. "I don't know where the seller is. The call sounded like it was being made on Aruba, though. I could hear island music in the background, though the voice disguiser he's using made the music sound very bad."

"I swear to God," Philip snapped. "I don't know why I'm paying you a commission. What if I don't want this to happen at the Alto Vista Chapel?"

"Look, man," the Chin answered cockily. "I'm making this work for you. You wanted the delivery to take place in Aruba. You got it. It's tomorrow, at 11:00. Alto Vista Chapel."

Philip cursed under his breath. "You're going to be there."

"Of course! I need to collect."

Philip hung up and stared at the phone for a couple more minutes. He'd been in this business long enough to develop a sixth sense about people—a kind of an alarm system.

That alarm was buzzing now. Loudly. Alto Vista Chapel represented a change in plan. That alarm was telling him that Lorenzo the Chin was trying to stick it to him. But Philip didn't know how.

Through the open door of the office, he saw the headlights of a car shine on the villa as it pulled in front. He knew Cy had left his car behind, so this would be their ride bringing them home. Relieved, he opened a hidden safe in the bottom drawer of the desk and slid in the silver briefcase. Quickly, he locked everything up.

Things hadn't gone too well with Morgan today. Somehow, he had to make it up to her. He sure as hell didn't want to lose her. Despite his crazy hours and the demands of his job, he loved having her around. Actually, it surprised him. Looking at her, listening to her, learning about her life and her interests and plans made him feel whole. He hadn't failed completely. His life wasn't totally empty. He was the father of a great kid . . . even if Jean did deserve most of the credit. Still, Morgan was his, too. She was the one good thing that had come out of his disaster of a marriage.

Philip wearily pushed to his feet and left the office. He could see the car headlights were out. Morgan still hadn't come in, though.

He'd thought some more about her relationship with Cy. He'd decided he had to just get over some of his worries. Kids grew up. Nowadays, they grew up earlier. At least, it seemed earlier.

Jean definitely didn't seem too worried about it. He'd been wound up enough tonight to locate a number for her in India. It had been around five in the morning her time when he'd called, and her new husband had answered the phone. Kabir had been a hell of a lot more gracious than Philip would have been: He'd just passed the phone over to Jean.

The former Mrs. Callahan had been her usual self, brusque and to the point. After he'd told her his concerns, she'd reminded him that Morgan was seventeen. She'd asked him if he remembered how old he was the first time he'd had sex. That had stopped him. Then she'd asked him how old the girl was that he'd had sex with. That finished him.

She'd told him he might consider trusting Morgan.

His first reaction had been, "Yeah. Maybe." After hanging up and thinking about it though, he realized she was right. He should trust his daughter.

Philip opened the sliding glass door and walked out into the dark courtyard. The car outside of the fence had been left running. He heard a knock on the guesthouse door, followed by a woman's voice calling softly.

He reached behind him and flipped the switch. The courtyard was immediately flooded with light.

"Morgan?" he called, walking toward the guesthouse.

"No, Mr. Callahan. It's Mackenzie Spencer." She stepped off Cy's porch into the light.

Philip was not exactly relieved to see the young woman alone. She and Morgan had gone off to the party together.

"Is Morgan back yet?" she asked before he could say anything.

"No. I thought she was at the party with you."

"She was." She glanced over her shoulder at the cottage. "How about Cy? Do you know if he's back?"

"I don't think so." He walked past her, and she fell in beside him. "My understanding was that Cy was meeting you two out there."

"He did," she replied in a small voice.

"Maybe I'm making too much out of nothing."

"What's going on?" he asked, stopping abruptly.

"Probably nothing," she said gently. "It's just that we'd planned to leave around midnight, but they'd disappeared. I just got worried, but that doesn't mean anything."

They were standing by the guesthouse door. Philip knocked on it a couple of times. Nothing. He doubted anyone was home. "When was the last time you saw them?"

"Around nine o'clock . . . at the party."

Four hours. Christ.

"Do you know where they went?"

"For a walk on the beach, I think," she said. "Morgan left her crutches behind, though."

Two young people on the beach. What could they be doing for four hours? A few things sprang to Philip's mind. He ran a hand down his face. Why in God's name had he ever brought up the subject of sex with either one of them?

"I'm feeling low about coming here and worrying you like this, sir," Mackenzie said quietly. "It's probably nothing, you know? The party is still going on. They're together. What could go wrong?"

That's right, Philip told himself. *They're together. What could go wrong?*

Chapter 25

The wood floor in the bathroom was rough and dirty. Not the kind of dirt that came from people using it. The dust and grit was from construction.

Morgan remembered when she was about twelve, she and a school friend had sneaked into a house that was being built in a lot in their neighborhood. The smell of the new wood and the wallboard made an impression on her. She could smell it now, too.

While she'd had that butterfly feeling in her stomach then because she was someplace she shouldn't have been, right now she had a cold stone about the size of a coconut sitting in her belly.

And with good reason, too, she thought. She and Cy had been kidnapped.

Cy had immediately put up a fight on the beach when their abductors appeared. With the cold muzzle of the gun pressed to Morgan's temple, Tony had explained that Cy had better cooperate or she was dead. The son of a U.S. senator was plenty enough collateral to serve their purpose. Morgan remembered Mackenzie's stories, and fear unlike anything she'd ever experienced washed through her. She had no doubt they would carry out their threat. She broke into a cold sweat, and her chest began to tighten, making it hard for her to breathe.

Cy's decision to stop fighting only brought slight relief, though. The creeps had dragged them to an SUV that was waiting not too far up the beach. Morgan had known right then the real danger was just starting.

She just couldn't figure out what they wanted.

She pulled at the duct tape they'd used to bind her hands and feet. There was no way she was going to free herself. While Tony held the gun, the goon had taped their hands behind their backs as soon as they arrived here.

She looked up at Cy. He'd succeeded in inching his way toward the small single window. The moon was just starting to shed some light through it.

"See anything?" she asked.

"Not yet." He moved to the side, trying to look from a different angle.

Tony had made them lie down on the car seat before throwing a blanket over them. She didn't know exactly where they were, but the drive hadn't taken too long. They had to be in the northern part of the island. She had a feeling they'd gone straight inland.

"There's another house about a hundred yards away to the left. It looks like it's still under construction, too. There is no sign of life anywhere."

"Perfect for holding us," she whispered. Tomorrow was Sunday, which meant nobody would be coming to work on the house. They could be held here for at least twenty-four hours.

A few minutes after they were dumped in here, she'd heard a car drive off. She had a feeling one of their abductors—probably the gorilla—was still downstairs, though. It wasn't a warm feeling.

Cy turned away from the window. She saw him look around the dark room. The tub was the only thing that was installed. The sink and the toilet were only holes and copper pipes coming out of the wall. There were stacks of tile in the corner. She knew what he was looking for—anything left behind by the people working on the place that he could use. There was nothing.

"Do you have any idea what time it is?" she asked.

"I don't know . . . maybe two or three o'clock."

"Cy, do you think anyone has figured out that we're missing?"

"Of course," he said, sliding down against the wall that had the water pipe for the toilet sticking out.

She saw him sit on the floor and try to rub the tape on the metal. "Nobody saw us being kidnapped," Morgan argued. "They might just assume . . . you know, you and I might be spending a romantic night on the beach."

"Well, this is pretty romantic, isn't it?"

"Yeah. It's a dream come true."

"Seriously, despite our disagreement, I think your father knows I wouldn't keep you out this late. At least, not without calling him."

After her own argument with Philip this afternoon, Morgan figured her father would probably think she was trying to teach him a lesson. She heard someone walking across a floor downstairs, and she tensed. The way Tony had been eyeing her dress and making comments before made her feel sick to her stomach. They were silent until the footsteps stopped.

"What do you think they want?" she whispered.

"I don't know," Cy answered. "It's not like we come from families famous for having lots of money. If they were going to take somebody, why us? I don't get it."

"Taking *us* wasn't random. They knew who you were."

"But so what? It's not like I'm a Kennedy or anything."

Morgan hadn't told him that she was probably the one responsible for endangering his life.

"There's something you should know," she said softly.

He recognized a change in her tone and stopped struggling with the pipe.

"The two creeps who kidnapped us, they know me, too. And I know them."

"You do?"

She quickly shook her head, recognizing her error. "I mean, I know *of* them. They were at The Brick Oven on Thursday. Mac gave me the lowdown on them."

"Who are they?"

"The younger guy is named Tony. He's supposedly the nephew of a criminal, middleman-type named Lorenzo the Chin."

"You've got to be kidding me. The guy's name is the Chin?"

"That's what Mac said . . . and she seemed to know what she was talking about."

"Okay, so what is it about us that would make the Chin want to grab us?"

"He was the jerk that was hassling me at the airport the afternoon you picked me up there."

Cy was silent for a moment. "I remember him. Kind of a scrawny guy. He backed right off as soon as you swung your crutch at me. But I still can't see why he'd want to come back after you or me."

"That day at the restaurant, when Mac and I saw them, Lorenzo was with these two other guys that she thought were Colombians and might be involved with drugs. And this is where everything gets ugly." She let out a shaky breath. "I think . . . I think we're here because of something that Philip is involved in, and I think they were planning to take me. I think you were just an unexpected bonus. You just happened to be in the wrong place at the wrong time. You heard that phone call Tony made from the car. From what I could understand, I think he was telling Lorenzo that there had been a change of plan . . . that he had the two of us."

"Philip is involved with these criminals?"

"Yeah."

"I don't know, Morgan," he said doubtfully. "Your father might have some job issues, but being mixed up with criminals seems a little far-fetched."

"I'm telling you, he is." Morgan leaned her back against the tub. "I know he knows them. I just don't know for sure if he's doing something wrong."

"I can't believe your father is—"

"There's all this mysterious evidence," she said, cutting him off. "Incriminating stuff. But I still want to trust him. I don't want to believe he'd knowingly do anything that would hurt me. Hurt us."

"What incriminating stuff?"

Morgan took a deep breath and started at the beginning, telling him about the five passports she'd found in his desk, about the private phone line in the office, and how he always spoke in a different language when she was listening to his conversations . . . like he was hiding something. Finally, she told Cy about seeing Philip getting into a car with the Colombians she'd seen with Lorenzo.

"The sad thing is that I confronted him with all of this yesterday. I told him what I knew. I gave him a chance to explain it. But he didn't. He just walked away." She fought back the tears that were gathering in her eyes. "What else am I going to believe except that he's mixed up in something illegal?"

Cy didn't say anything for the longest moment. He stretched his legs out in front of him.

"Have you ever thought that your father might not be telling people the truth about his job?"

"Since I've been here, yes. But before

that . . . ?" Morgan looked at him across the dark room. "I don't know. Before this trip to Aruba, I hadn't seen him for three years. Why?"

"Because of something I've suspected about my own father."

"What do you mean?" She was all ears.

"Despite what I was told about him having a desk job in finance, I've had a suspicion that he actually worked in the field, as a spy."

"You mean, like he was working for the CIA?" she whispered, stunned.

"I think so."

"But how did you find out? Did he tell you about it?"

"No, never. But there were enough clues." Cy said. "Odd things, some of them as strange as the passports you discovered in Philip's desk. But I think the final thing that convinced me happened about six months before he left the job. He was supposedly doing an audit of some government office in Idaho. My mom got a call one night. A car came and they flew her to Turkey to visit him in a hospital."

"Was he sick?"

"I wasn't supposed to know, but she was a wreck when she was leaving. She was almost hysterical. I pried it out of her that he'd been wounded."

"Tough audit," Morgan said quietly.

He shook his head. "My father and Philip started working together. I think Philip might be in the same business. He doesn't have five passports and different identities because he's making a buck on the side working with drug dealers. There's something much bigger involved."

"And I screwed it up," she said, horrified.

"What do you mean by that?"

"That first day at the airport, I told Lorenzo my father is a high-ranking official for the United States government. I thought he was just a boring clerk. I might have exposed him to his enemies."

"You can't blame yourself for that." Cy lowered his voice. "The important thing to remember is that if all of our assumptions are right and Philip is CIA or in some other government agency, then at least we have a chance. Creeps like these guys are not going to outsmart him."

Morgan hoped Cy was right. At the same time, she couldn't stop the guilt piling up for all the doubts she'd had about her father. He deserved better.

More than anything right now, she wished she could get a second chance.

Chapter 26

I left Leiter there, sir. He's trying to get close enough to have a look into the party."

Philip stared over the roof of the white car at the dark windows of the guesthouse. He fixed his gaze on the driver again. "You're sure they didn't get by you . . . They didn't leave with someone else?"

The driver shook his head. "No, sir. We had a good spot to watch the door of the villa. Everyone was coming and going through that door. We saw the two friends leave, but they left without your daughter and Cy. I think they're still in the house."

"What makes you think that?"

"When I left to drive here, there were still eight cars outside the residence. The band was still there, though the music had stopped. They were still partying, sir."

In his entire career, Philip had never run an operation in his own backyard. He'd never allowed the risk of his own family getting involved.

Not until this summer. This weekend.

He'd had two of his operatives keeping an eye on Morgan for the past couple of days. They had specific orders to be discreet, but to make sure no harm came her way.

"And you think Morgan and the senator's son are still in that beach house in Malmok."

"Yes, sir. They didn't leave by the front door. We would have seen them."

"What about the beach itself?" He could see the agent squirm slightly in the seat of the white car. "Tell me you had sight of the beach."

The driver looked straight ahead. "No, sir. We didn't. There was no way to watch the beach without drawing attention."

They could still be in the villa. They could have gone down the beach for privacy and returned after Mackenzie and Nick left the party. They could be sitting in a dark corner somewhere. They could be in one of the villa's bedrooms, for all he knew.

Still, something wasn't right. It was getting late. Very late. Never mind about calling dear old dad. They weren't so thoughtless that they wouldn't let their friends know where they were.

Philip drummed his fingers on the top of the car. He wasn't sure this was the type of thing that Morgan had ever done before. He knew Jean wouldn't appreciate it if he called her again tonight asking. He wouldn't do that to her anyway. Long-distance parenting was hell. She'd taken care of so many crises on her own, understanding how helpless he'd be from afar. It was his turn.

Besides, Aruba was a very safe island. He'd have reason to be a lot more worried if she was this late coming home in Boston or D.C.

No, he had to trust her. He had no choice. Not with what he had going on in the morning. Philip had too much on his plate right now to worry about her. He had to focus on what he had in front of him. There was too much at stake.

"You want me to check the beach, sir?"

"Yes, I do. I want you to find out if they're inside that house or if they're on that beach. I want you to contact me with any information you have. But I want you to watch the house for only another hour."

"You want us back here, then?"

"No, I need you to go to the Alto Vista Chapel."

"You changed the drop point?"

"*They* did. We need to get there early and set up before anybody shows up." Philip put both hands on the driver's door. "You and Leiter need to be in position somewhere in the area. Lorenzo is acting a little funny, and we need to cover ourselves."

"We'll be ready, sir."

"Right," Philip said, trying to sound more confident than he felt. "You have one hour at the beach house. Find those two kids."

"They're back," Cy whispered from the window. "The Jaguar and another car just pulled up."

"Great," Morgan said tiredly, stretching her neck from side to side. Every part of her body was either numb or aching. While leaning against Cy, she'd dozed off for a few minutes around dawn. But he'd been up and working himself toward the window soon after that.

"That weasel, Tony, brought company this time."

"Who is it?"

"Your friend Lorenzo the Chin is with him. There's also a guy who looks like a clone of the goon who was with Tony."

Morgan remembered him, too. A tremor ran through her as Mackenzie's words rushed back. These guys were bad to the bone.

"I'm afraid," she whispered.

Cy turned to her. "Don't be. We're gonna need every ounce of our courage. We have to work our way out of this."

Morgan noticed that he wasn't referring to someone else coming and rescuing them anymore. She wondered if he was losing hope, too.

Voices echoed through the house. Someone was coming up the stairs. Cy moved away from the window and worked himself close to her before sliding down to the floor. The door opened, and Tony walked in, carrying something folded under one arm.

He looked from one to the other, a grin on his face. They were sitting a couple of feet apart. "Come on. I only tied your hands and feet. I expected you two lovebirds would have made the most of what might be your last night together."

"Why don't you keep your scum-sucking mouth shut?" Cy spat out.

"Nice manners, college boy. Maybe I should shut *your* mouth."

"¡Vamos! Tony!" Lorenzo shouted from downstairs. "We can't be late."

Tony tossed what he had under his arm onto Morgan's lap. It looked like a dress. "Wear this. We don't want you looking like you just came from a beauty pageant."

"I'm sure that's going to happen," she answered.

"Just change, Red."

"And how am I supposed to do that with my wrists taped together?" she argued.

"No problem. I'll do it for you." Tony took a step toward her as Lorenzo shouted to him again.

When he hesitated, she knew she had to make use of the opportunity. "I need to go to the bathroom . . . bad!"

Tony scowled and took a folding knife out of his pocket. Morgan tried not to wince as he grabbed her roughly by the arms and stood her up. Two quick slashes and her hands were free. But she had no feeling in them.

"Change," he ordered.

"My feet, too," she told him, forcing herself to gather all her courage. "And I have to use the bathroom."

"Use this one," he said motioning to the drainpipe in the floor. It was plugged with a rag.

"Have it your way, I'll pee in the dress." She picked it up off the floor.

A string of words she thought were both Spanish and Papiamento came from downstairs. Morgan had no doubt they were profanities.

"*¡Vaya con diablo!*" Tony cursed. "You're a pain in the ass, you know that?"

He leaned down and slashed at the tape that bound her left ankle to the cast on her right foot.

"Come with me." He pushed her roughly out the door.

When they went downstairs, she saw Lorenzo standing by a window in the front room dialing a number on his cell phone. A feeling of nausea hit her as the Chin looked over at her and leered. He mouthed the words, "You're mine," before turning his attention back to the call.

She was relieved Tony steered her through a half-finished kitchen, where she saw the two gorillas standing at a counter and eating fast-food breakfast sandwiches. It was a lot easier complaining to Tony than it would be to Lorenzo. Maybe it was the Chin's age, or maybe it was the fact that she knew he'd carved a bloody path to make himself what he was. Whatever, she knew she wouldn't get much compassion from the older man.

As they went down a short hallway, Morgan realized that Tony had left the door open for Cy. Not that he could go anywhere, she thought.

There was a half bathroom next to the kitchen. This one had a toilet installed, but there was no water in it.

"This will have to do," Tony said, pushing her in and closing the door. "Hurry up."

Morgan changed quickly. The dress they'd given her was a plain green uniform—like one a hotel employee would wear. She figured they must have stolen it. But she didn't care. She much preferred to go around in something like this rather than the risqué dress she had worn for the party. She went to the bathroom.

Tony banged on the door. "Hurry up."

Morgan's cast crunched on something on the floor. She looked down. It was a thin piece of broken mirror. She picked it up and slid it carefully inside her cast.

Coming out of the bathroom, she heard Lorenzo's voice. He was talking to someone on the phone in English.

"I'll have the files by noon," he said. "*Sí*, I'll fly out this afternoon. You can have the auction tomorrow. Guaranteed. I have insurance." There was a pause. "*Sí*, his daughter and the son of a senator." Pause. "Callahan will do business. He has no choice."

Chapter 27

The bright yellow Alto Vista Chapel sat in the center of an open area atop a rocky hill overlooking the blue Caribbean. A low stone wall formed a perfect square around the tiny chapel. Each side of the square measured exactly one hundred feet long. Within the square, mustard-yellow benches had been laid out in four concentric semicircles that radiated from the two wide wooden doors. The doors opened to reveal the colorful interior of the chapel and the carved oak altar.

Outside of the wall, narrow roads led back toward the little village of Noord. Aside from a few houses situated some distance from the chapel, though, the place was isolated.

In short, Philip thought as he looked around him, it was a security nightmare.

The sun was already hot and the sky was as blue as Dutch tile. The breeze coming in from the sea swirled around him as he walked to where the techies were putting the finishing touches on the video and audio devices that would capture the event about to take place. Everything was wireless, of course. Three small cameras, no larger than pens, would take in the entire area, as well as focus in on the bench where the delivery would be made. Two had been positioned on the roof of the chapel, and one on the hinge of one of chapel doors. Two more had been placed outside the stone walls.

Technicians were wiring the two men that had been posing as Colombians. Philip himself was already wired.

Everyone had been playing their part perfectly so far. If the renegade agent Philip and his group had been working to ferret out for eight months had been on the island for any length of time, then he would only have seen Lorenzo wining and dining them. A perfectly natural activity.

Something was going on with Lorenzo, though. Philip could feel it. In his mind he went through the steps of the operation, trying to see if he'd missed anything.

For more than a year, Homeland Security had been getting reports that a renegade agent was operating within the Agency. Whoever it was, he was selling information about individual CIA operatives working undercover across the globe. When rumors began to surface that the traitor was looking for a buyer for a master list of operations in South America, Philip had been called in. Word was that the list contained not only the identities of hundreds of operatives working in South America, but also their defined missions and their connections inside a dozen governments.

A plan was formulated. Rumors were circulated that Philip, who had earlier been in Colombia, was being informally investigated for "inappropriate behavior." The rumors were vague about what he was suspected of doing, but he was immediately transferred to Aruba, where he was to pose as an Energy Department bureaucrat stationed there.

There, the plan called for Philip to "acquire" a shady middleman who had a history of brokering deals with South American drug cartels. That middleman, Lorenzo the Chin, bought into the scheme immediately. The U.S. government would pay him half a million dollars simply to broker the deal.

Lorenzo immediately put out word that he

had a buyer for information about CIA operations in South America. His buyers, who would appear to be Colombians, would actually be CIA operatives. Their cover was that they were going to sell the information to interested parties from Caracas to Valparaiso.

It didn't take long for word to come back to Lorenzo. The transfer of information for money could occur in Aruba—off American soil—while funds were wired to an account in the Caymans.

As the time grew closer to the sale, Lorenzo notified the seller that the Colombian buyers were hesitant to transfer the hefty price without some verification that the list was genuine. The South Americans were demanding a way to verify the information they were buying.

Philip was their man for that.

The trap was laid. The fake Colombians would fly in to oversee the deal. Philip would meet the seller in a public place. The seller would pass on the list to Philip, who would verify its accuracy and tell the buyers to transfer the money. The seller would be in communication with his banker via cell phone.

What the seller would not know, however,

is that Philip's people would be recording the entire transaction, and as soon as the renegade agent went back to the United States, Homeland Security and the FBI would be there to arrest him. Collecting evidence was not ordinarily the CIA's function, but this was not an ordinary case. Flushing this turncoat would preserve the safety of countless agents in South America.

"Let's go, people," he shouted. "We need everyone out of here now."

The religious service was at 11:00.

He glanced at his watch. Pulling out his cell phone, he dialed the villa. Nothing. He called the guesthouse next. Nothing. He'd found Morgan's phone on her dresser. So much for taking it with her. He shook his head and put the phone away.

He was going to have to kill the two of them, pure and simple.

Within fifteen minutes the site was cleared — with the exception of himself and the "Colombian" buyers, who were sitting in their stretch limo.

A battered construction trailer containing monitors and communication devices had been positioned a half mile from the chapel. There would be other operatives in the congregation, but they would only act if the entire plan went to pieces.

He thought through the plan one more time and took a deep breath.

They were ready. As he looked at the open doors of the chapel, though, he wished he'd said a prayer. He had a feeling they were all going to need it.

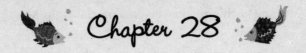

Chapter 28

The Jaguar pulled in around the traffic and parked behind a black limo in the circular driveway of the Alto Vista Chapel. Morgan looked through the tinted-glass windows at the large group of people who'd gathered for the Sunday service. Most of the benches outside were full, and there were a few people sitting on the stone walls that went around the place. She spotted Lorenzo and one of his gorillas sitting on the last bench, close to the stone wall. They appeared to be saving a few seats between them.

Morgan searched the audience for her father. She thought she saw him sitting a couple of rows in front of Lorenzo, next to the two Colombians. They were seated toward the outside end of the bench. She bumped Cy with her shoulder. He nodded. He'd seen Philip, too.

She hoped Cy was right about everything. She wanted to believe that Philip was doing the right thing. That he was on the right side of the law.

More than anything, though, she hoped he would kick Lorenzo's butt and rescue her and Cy.

Tony had left the car running. The windows were closed, the air-conditioning blasting. The goon next to him in the passenger seat took out his gun and started screwing an extension to the end of the weapon.

"Silencer," Tony said, grinning at her in the mirror. "Sometimes a job must be done quiet."

When they put them in the car to bring them here, Tony had cut the duct tape off Cy's legs, too. Thanks to Morgan's whining, they'd taped their hands in front of them. On the way to the chapel, she'd been able to reach inside her cast, pull out the shard of mirror, and slide it into Cy's hands. Since then, she'd seen him position it under his leg and work on cutting through the tape binding his wrists whenever the two in front weren't looking. She didn't look at him, but she knew he was working at it now.

"Are we getting out?" Cy asked irritably from next to her.

"Not right now, college boy," Tony told him.

"I have to go to the bathroom," Morgan whined.

"*¡Jesucristo!* You went back at the house."

"I have to go again," she said persistently.

"Well, you have to wait."

Cy's elbows moved and bumped her. Her arguing was giving him a chance to work faster.

"How long?" she asked.

"Until I say you can get out of the car."

"Nice leather seats," she commented. "Sorry I'll be messing up the interior of such a nice car."

"You are truly the biggest pain in my ass, you know that?"

"How long do I have to wait?" she pressed.

"I don't know. Maybe half an hour. Mass is starting right now."

"I can't wait till Mass is over."

"You don't have to wait that long, Red. If your papa cooperates, you'll be back in his arms long before Mass is over."

Morgan looked at Cy. That meant they had very little time.

"Mind if we sit here?" a woman's voice whispered.

Philip looked up at the two young tourists

who were standing at the end of the row, waiting for him to move the newspaper.

"Yeah, I do," he said shortly. "You can't sit here."

For a second, he thought the guy was going to argue. But then, he seemed to think it over, and they moved off.

Philip glanced at his watch. It was 11:10. The service had started, but there was still no sign of him.

A shadow moved over the seat. He looked up. Another woman, this one wearing a broad-brimmed black hat and sunglasses. There was little of her face visible.

"The seat is taken," he said.

"Yes, I know." She leaned down and picked up the newspaper. "Thank you for holding it for me."

Philip looked at the woman. He didn't know her. He wasn't even sure that he was dealing with his contact until she opened a large bag on her lap and pulled out a small electronic device. It was a hand-held computer. She passed it to him.

"Everything is here," she said in a low voice.

Philip wondered if she was the renegade

agent, or the spouse or girlfriend of someone on the inside. One thing was certain, though, they wouldn't be getting a good picture of her face. He took a cell phone out of his pocket.

"How do I work it?" he whispered, juggling the cell phone in his other hand.

She leaned toward him. "Let me show you."

The phone in Philip's hand fell on her lap. She picked it up and handed to him. He let it sit between them on the bench.

With her help, he opened the file and started scanning through the names on the spreadsheet. She'd organized it alphabetically. Actual names and aliases of operatives, along with addresses, phone numbers, latest assignments. Some of them he knew. It was a death sentence for every operative on the list. He went to the *C*s. His name was first on the list. All the information was accurate, with the exception of this assignment. Only the Director of the CIA and two high-ranking members of Homeland Security knew his real mission.

He turned to the "buyers" and nodded.

The one next to Philip leaned toward the seller, whispering, "How do we know this is the only copy you're selling?"

"You have my word," she said in a low voice.

"Honor among thieves?" Philip murmured.

"You and I are the same kind of people, Mr. Callahan." She lowered her glasses slightly to look into his face. Her eyes were blue. "Not thieves, just entrepreneurs. We make the most of our opportunities."

"Is this a one-time deal, or can we look forward to doing business in the future?" the other "buyer" asked.

"I'm definitely building this business. By September, I'll be putting on an auction for a similar list"—her voice was barely audible now—"of the operatives in the Middle East. That one will be a very high-ticket item, but you're welcome to join the bidding."

"I am certainly interested," the same agent whispered.

"The transfer of money, gentlemen?"

Philip picked up his cell phone and dialed. His contact answered.

"We couldn't pick up her fingerprints the first time she touched the phone," said the operative at the other end. "Have her handle it again."

Philip made himself look very annoyed. "You had her account number. Here she is, she can tell you the number herself." He handed the phone to her. "Sorry."

She stared at him for a moment, then took the phone. Opening a folded paper in her bag, she quickly read the numbers for the account the money was to be transferred into. She handed the phone back to him.

Philip spoke into the phone. "Everything all set?"

"Bingo. It's a she and not a he. We have *her*." The agent on the phone rattled off her name, the department, the personal information they had on file on her. "Now let her swim away. We'll have a warrant for her arrest in hand by the time she arrives back in the good old U.S. of A."

Philip ended the call. "It's all set."

She took out her own cell phone and dialed her bank. Everything was as expected. She nodded.

"Nice doing business with you, gentlemen." She got up and walked away.

She'd be tailed while she was in Aruba. Of

course, there was still a chance that she'd escape and never return to the States, but that was a chance they had to take. The important thing was that they had the list.

Philip felt himself tense up as Lorenzo slid onto the bench next to him. He said nothing to the middleman, but picked up the silver briefcase from the ground by his feet and handed it to him.

Lorenzo took it and opened the briefcase slightly. He closed it and snapped the latches shut. He stretched his hand toward Philip. "Now, the list."

"What do you mean?"

"Keep your voice down," Lorenzo hissed. "And don't try to stall and give the rest of your spy friends time to arrive. My man has strict instructions."

He motioned with his head toward the back. Philip looked and his blood froze in his veins.

Morgan was standing by the black Jag. One of Lorenzo's thugs was standing next to her, his right hand hidden behind her back. There was no question in Philip's mind that the goon was holding a gun on her.

"I'm taking that list, and then I'll give you your daughter and the senator's son." Lorenzo reached for the hand-held computer. "A fair trade, don't you think?"

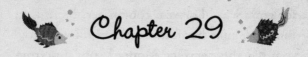

Chapter 29

The Jag's windows facing the chapel were open.

Before they'd made her get out of the car, Morgan had seen a woman come and talk to Philip and then leave. When Lorenzo moved up to sit beside her father, though, Tony cut the tape off her wrists and told her to get out of the Jaguar. The gorilla kept a hand on her arm and now stood next to her, jabbing the gun into her back. She was shaking inside, and she had no clue what was going on. Whatever it was, though, she knew she was being used to get something from Philip.

And all the while, Mass just continued along. The priest was standing at the lectern giving a sermon in English and Papiamento.

"Do you really have to jab that thing into me?" she complained, knowing she had to somehow ruin whatever Porcupine Butt was engineering here.

Philip turned around at that moment and

looked at her. Lorenzo continued to speak to him. She gave her father a slight wave.

"Don't be nervous, Morgan," Cy said from behind her. "You know what that does to you."

"You shut up," Tony said from the front seat.

"Deep breath, Morgan. Don't let them get to you," Cy continued.

She got what he was saying. Asthma attack.

Morgan drew a deep breath and then another.

"Don't be scared. Just keep breathing."

"What's going on?" she heard Tony ask.

She forced herself to cough a couple of times. Then she started taking deep painful breaths in short succession.

"Cool it." The gun dug harder into her back.

"I can't . . . I can't breathe," she managed to say.

"The stress gets to her," Cy said urgently. "She has asthma. She needs her inhaler or she's going to pass out."

"Bring her back inside the car," Tony ordered.

It was too late. Morgan staggered forward a step, acting woozy, coughing a little bit more.

"Help me," she gasped as loud as she could. "I can't breathe."

She half turned to see the gorilla scrambling to hide the gun in his belt. Tony was trying to get his door opened. She stumbled toward the wall, obviously struggling for air.

The back two rows of people had turned and were looking at her. She heard the car doors open and decided the moment had come. She went down on her face in a pretend faint.

Tony and the goon rushed toward her. Cy gave one last slash with the shard of mirror and felt the tape give. He yanked his hands free. They were a bloody mess, but he didn't care. He reached over the seat, grabbed the keys out of the ignition and shoved his door open.

Coming around the car, he pegged the keys as hard as he could over the chapel roof. They flashed in the sunlight as they flew out of sight. He wasn't going to make it easy for them to get Morgan out of here, even if they did drag her back to the Jag.

It was unbelievable, but the priest was still talking. He wasn't taking any notice of the commotion they were creating.

Tony and his goon were trying to peel Morgan off the road.

"Call for help. This girl is dying," Cy yelled from the top of his lungs, running toward them.

As Tony turned, Cy put his shoulder right into the scumbag's face, slamming him into the gorilla and sending all three of them sprawling into the dirt beyond Morgan.

Morgan heard Cy yell and then felt the wind when he blasted into the creeps who were pawing at her. The big one let go of her, but the collision knocked her a couple of feet along the ground. As the men sailed over her, she felt herself roll up against the low wall, her cast cracking hard against the stone.

She wondered if her prayers would be heard, considering the fact that she was lying outside of the wall.

Chaos had broken out inside the chapel yard. Shouts and fighting quickly put an end to the Mass, and she could hear the priest yelling in Papiamento. Several women were shrieking, a baby was crying, and soon people were jumping over the stone wall near her and running off.

She figured with her limited mobility, it was safest all the way around if she just stayed where she was. She heard cars racing into the parking lot, the sound of sirens in the distance, and then the horns of cars trying to leave soon drowned out almost everything else.

Within minutes, though, the brawl subsided, and she felt someone rolling her onto her back. Morgan blinked her eyes as the priest, still wearing his green vestments, tried to put the mask of a portable oxygen tank over her mouth.

"No, wait! I—" She didn't get the next word out before the mask descended.

As she tried to push the priest's hand away, another face appeared over the clergyman's shoulder. It was her father.

"Morgan!"

She succeeded in getting the mask off her face and reached up.

"I'm so sorry," she whispered as he gathered her into his arms. "I didn't know what was going on. I thought you were—"

"It's okay, Morgan," he said, holding her. "Everything's okay."

She looked around wildly. "Where's Cy?"

"He's right there. My men are just checking out the cuts on his hands."

"And Lorenzo?"

"You can't see them from here, but he and his thugs are lying on their faces over there, handcuffed and waiting for the Aruban police to take them away. Kidnapping is a serious crime, especially here in Aruba." Philip pushed the hair out of her face. "I was worried about you. Are you hurt?"

She pressed her face against his chest. "No, Dad. Not anymore."

Chapter 30

"$\mathcal{W}$ith everything you have going on, I can't believe you're missing work for this," Morgan told her father as they sat waiting for the X-ray technician to develop and read her films.

"Hey, there's nowhere else I'd rather be right now."

Morgan felt her throat tighten at his words. She looped an arm through his as they sat in the hospital waiting room.

"Still, you didn't have to. I mean, I have to come back on Thursday, anyway."

"I'll come back then, too."

"But how are you making out with all that mess from yesterday?"

"Actually, things are going pretty smoothly," he said.

"Can you tell me about it?"

"No."

"Will you *ever* tell me what happened?"

"Probably not."

"Will you at least tell me that Lorenzo and

his creepo goons have been put away?"

"The Aruban authorities have seen to that. They're not going to see the light of day for a long, long time."

She gave him a narrow stare. "Will you tell me what kind of business dealings you had with him?"

Philip held her hand. "Don't ask, baby. I can't tell you."

It didn't matter if he told her. They'd crossed a threshold yesterday.

Morgan thought about how far they'd come. She trusted him. She no longer thought that he was involved in illegal activities. He didn't want to mess up his life or their relationship. She knew she meant a lot to her father. She had a feeling that he, too, understood that in her mind they were once again a family.

Morgan still couldn't resist, though. She leaned toward him and lowered her voice. "Answer just one question."

He tried to look suspicious, but she could see the traces of a smile. "What?"

"Are you a spy?"

"You have a one-track mind."

"You're welcome to call me stubborn," she

said with a smile. "I get it from my father."

Philip looked down the hall and stood up. "Forget about the technician. Apparently, the orthopedist is here, too."

"I'm going to keep after you until I have an answer," she warned him, standing up, as well.

The X rays looked excellent. The orthopedist's opinion was that there was no point in waiting until Thursday. The cast could come off today. Morgan was thrilled.

"Last day of using them," Philip told her, looking at the crutches as they went down the hall. "You can leave them here."

"Actually, I'm going to take these with me."

"Planning on breaking your leg again?"

"No, they're a gift for a good friend."

Morgan saw him shoot her a quick look.

"He won't need them," he said quietly as they reached the treatment room.

She stopped and reached up to press a kiss on his cheek.

"Thanks, Dad."

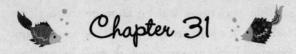

Chapter 31

Six weeks later

Morgan knew these couple of hours they were spending at the Natural Pool would probably be the last she and Cy would have together alone before she flew back to Boston tomorrow.

Jean and her new husband were back home, and she'd been calling every day, insisting that Morgan come back ten days earlier than originally planned. To Morgan's shock, her father had gone along with it, too. Both of them had used excuses about the change of school and registration and getting ready.

Morgan was fed up with all of it. She didn't want to go. It was only the first week of August. Three weeks before school started. Neither of them were giving her a chance, though. Philip was booting her out. Here's your ticket, see you later.

And frankly, it hurt. She thought they were having a great summer together. She *knew* they were.

"Do you think it'll be another three years before I see him again?" she asked Cy as they climbed back up on a smooth rock ledge. The pool was formed by rocky outcroppings fifteen feet high or more. Much of the rock had been smoothed by eons of tidal surges, and the pool was deep and blue and clear.

"No," Cy said, taking her snorkeling equipment and putting it with his on the rocks. "I don't think either of you would let that happen."

"But it could be," she said sadly. "He won't let me ask any questions about what he's doing next or where he's going. It's like I can't even call him and say, 'Hey Dad, can I come and visit this weekend?'"

"Why not?" He reached over and tucked a strand of wet hair behind her ear. "I think you should do exactly that. Keep him on his toes."

"Yeah. Sure. I'm sure he'd just love to have me create another disaster for him in Liechtenstein or Slovakia or Laos or Bangladesh or wherever he's going."

"You didn't create any disasters. Everything worked out exactly the way they planned it. I believe his operation was a great success."

"How do you know that?" she asked suspiciously.

"Oh, you know how it is. It's a guy thing. Male bonding and all that."

"That's not fair." She shoved him, and he slid all the way down into the water.

When he didn't surface immediately, Morgan scrambled down to the edge.

"Cy!" she yelled.

At that moment, he surged up and grabbed her ankle, dragging her into the water with him.

"Ouch! Coral sting! That hurt!" she sputtered as she surfaced. "You are such a brute."

"You started it."

"You didn't have to retaliate," she scolded. "I'm leaving tomorrow. You should let me get away with things for a change."

"You really think so?" he asked, gathering Morgan against him.

She nodded, liking the way he looked at her, the way his hands were sliding over her body.

"What should I let you get away with now?" he asked hoarsely.

Morgan looked around. They were still the

only two in the pool.

"I'll just settle for this." She wrapped her arms around his neck and kissed him deeply.

Waves crashed over the rock barrier at the ocean side of the pool and sprayed over them. Warm water washed around them, pushing their bodies even closer until they might have been molded out of one flesh.

This would be the most painful part. Walking away from Cy. Morgan was in love with him. It was that simple. And she believed him when he said he felt the same way about her. For so many weeks, they'd practically been inseparable. Having her cast off had given her the freedom to explore the island. She and Cy had done all the things she couldn't do before. Swimming. Snorkeling. She'd even taken classes in scuba diving, and he'd taught her to windsurf.

They'd had so much fun.

They'd only had to give a sworn statement to the court magistrate. There was no getting out on bail for Lorenzo here in Aruba. He was in for the duration, and knowing that, Morgan felt so much safer as she and Cy roamed the island. She'd been even more relieved when she read in the newspaper that the Chin was sentenced to a lengthy prison term.

But now, her summer was over. She hadn't left yet, and she was already missing Cy.

Tears trickled down her lashes, and he kissed them away. He cupped her face, his green eyes looking into hers.

"Don't. We're not going to do this, remember? Two weeks. That's all. I'm coming to Boston to see you in two weeks."

He'd told her that before. "It isn't the next time that we see each other that worries me, but the times after that."

"We're going to work it out, Morgan."

"Do you know, there are four hundred forty-seven and sixty-three hundredths of a mile between Boston and Washington?"

"You've been checking, huh?"

She nodded. "Mapquest. And that's going the shortest route."

He laughed, gathering her tight against his chest. He pressed a kiss on her forehead. "It only takes an hour or so to Logan Airport from Washington."

"But there's the driving to the airport, and

the driving time back. You might get tired of it."

"I'll never get tired of it, Morgan." His hands rubbed her back, caressed her hair. He lifted her chin and this time the kiss was hotter.

Morgan responded. She could feel the sexual heat between their bodies rise. Suddenly, he broke off the kiss.

"We have to get back to the cottage."

"Why?" she asked shyly.

"So I can put some of that aloe cream on your back. You're getting burned again."

"Tanned."

"Right. But we can't let you get too tanned." He lifted her out of the water and onto the rocks. He climbed out behind her.

She knew they had to get to somewhere safe. This was the way their passion ran. Hot, explosive. They both worked at being careful, though.

A good choice, too, she thought as they picked up their towels and shoes. She could see a group of tourists just starting down the long path from the parking lot at the top of the cliff. They were heading for the Natural Pool.

Cy picked up their snorkeling equipment and held them with his towel in front of him.

Morgan couldn't help but laugh and wrapped a towel around her before walking up ahead of Cy on the winding path back toward the car.

They passed the tourists on a long set of stairs going up the side of the cliff. They exchanged some pleasantries about the beautiful weather and the breezes and temperature of the water as they went by.

At the car, Morgan peeled off the towel and put it on her seat. She was searching for her sundress when Cy came up behind her. He ran a finger just under the strap of her bikini top.

"You're definitely getting too much sun today. I won't forgive myself if after all these weeks you end up with sun poisoning."

She turned in his arms and kissed his chin. "I think we finished the tube of aloe yesterday afternoon in the guesthouse," she whispered. "Maybe we should stop on the way home and get some more?"

He reached around her and grabbed a drugstore bag from the backseat. She peeked inside. He was definitely prepared . . . and not just with aloe lotion. The only thing she asked for now was that the two of them be given some privacy for at least the rest of the morning.

And maybe some of the afternoon.

Morgan got only part of her wish.

They were able to get back home and showered together in her bathroom . . . for old times' sake. That was where she'd gotten stuck and Cy had seen her naked for the first time. They both wanted another memory to add to that one.

The phone was ringing as she stepped out of the shower.

It was Mackenzie's mother, reminding Morgan that she had to come by to pick up her last paycheck. No sooner had she hung up when Jean called from Boston, asking for the fifth time about Morgan's flight schedule. While on the phone, Morgan's mother started getting very philosophical about familial love and friendship and paths in life . . . and on and on. Morgan figured this had to be the effect of her summer immersion in Hindu culture.

Morgan didn't know if she should be thankful or angry at Kabir.

The next call was from Nick. He wanted to talk to Cy.

Morgan was suspicious about Mac and Nick and Cy having something in the works for tonight. She'd be a good sport and go along with it, but as much as she liked her friends and wanted to spend time with them, she had more faith that she'd be seeing them more often than her father. Mackenzie was talking about going to college in San Francisco, and they'd both promised to visit her during a school break.

No, what she really wanted to do was spend a little time with Philip.

Cy motioned for her to not eavesdrop. She made a face at him and poured couple of tall glasses of iced tea and headed out onto the courtyard.

She didn't want to be staring at suitcases now. She was in no mood to pack. What she wanted was to breathe the flower-scented air and see the beauty of Aruba and fill her senses with it. This had undoubtedly been the best summer of her life, and she didn't know when she'd be back on this island paradise again.

"Move, Fred," Morgan said, shooing away

the resident two-foot iguana she and Cy had named during the summer. She put the glasses on the table and sat down on one of the chairs in the shade. About five minutes later, she was surprised to hear Philip's car pull in on the other side of the wall. She got up to greet her father as he came through the gate.

"It's barely noon. How could they let you out of work this early?"

"It's Friday. I figured if my assistant can take the entire day off to hang around with my daughter, the least I could do was to take a half day off." He gave her a hug.

"That's wonderful," Morgan said, truly meaning it.

He put his briefcase on one of the chairs and eyed the two glasses of iced tea.

"Have some," she said. "I just brought them out."

He drank one of the glasses right down. There was something about him that she couldn't put her finger on. There was an excitement that hovered right beneath the surface. This was something new.

"Let me guess. You finished something important?"

He nodded and smiled.

"And everything worked out as you planned?"

He nodded again.

"That's wonderful, Dad," Morgan said happily. "You should celebrate. Do something special."

"*We'll* do something special," he corrected, looking around the courtyard. "Where's Cy?"

"Running up your phone bill. He kicked me out of the villa. I think he's planning something devious with Mackenzie and Nick for tonight."

Cy opened the sliding glass door and walked out. She noticed he was bringing out the pitcher of iced tea and an extra glass. She figured he must have seen Philip arrive.

"How did everything work out?" he asked Philip after an initial greeting.

"Perfect," her father answered.

"And the time frame?"

"Just as I told you."

"You two are speaking in code. That male bonding stuff again, isn't it?" Morgan complained. "Well, before you guys break out into spitting contests and flatten beer cans on your foreheads, remember that I'm leaving tomorrow. So good manners, gentlemen."

Philip and Cy grinned at each other. What the heck was going on?

"I'm going inside to make another pitcher of iced tea," Cy said, putting what he was carrying on the table and backing up.

"What's wrong with this?" she asked.

"I'm pretty thirsty," Philip said, pouring himself another glass. "Why don't you sit down, Morgan?"

She noticed a special look Cy sent her before disappearing into the villa. She couldn't decipher it.

"Sit down, Morgan," Philip repeated.

Suddenly, she was nervous. "No, I'm not going to sit down," she announced. "Come on. Out with it. What's going on?"

"Okay, well, *I* need to sit." Philip sat down and drank more tea.

"Dad, start talking. You're going to tell me something, so out with it. But I'm warning you. This had better not be bad news. I'm feeling pretty fragile right now, after being rejected and sent back to Jean ten days early. . . ."

"Morgan . . ."

"In fact, I still think it's totally unfair. . . ."

"Morgan, how would you like to come and live with me?"

"I mean, after not seeing me for . . ." She stopped and stared at him in disbelief, his words finally registering. "You want me to come live with you?"

"Yeah, I do."

"Where?"

"In Washington," he said.

She sat down but missed the chair.

As she went sprawling on the ground, her father immediately jumped out of his seat and was beside her. Cy must have been standing by the door, because he was there in an instant, too.

"Are you okay?"

She held on to both sets of hands as they lifted her to her feet. This time she sat gracefully on the edge of the seat. She looked up at Cy.

"Does he mean Washington, Ohio?"

"No."

"Washington, Saudi Arabia?"

Cy smiled at her and shook his head.

Morgan looked in confusion at Philip. He

pulled a chair close to hers and sat down.

"I'm taking a real desk job in Washington, D.C., at the end of the summer. And this won't be a three-month or six-month assignment. It's permanent, or at least for as long as I decide to continue working for the government. I could actually retire in a year."

Morgan's head swam with all this information. "When are you moving?"

"In two weeks."

"Does Jean know about this?"

He nodded. "I've been talking to her about it over the past couple of weeks."

"Was this her idea? I mean, me moving in with you?"

"No," he said firmly. "It's my idea . . . and she's already said flat out that she's not too happy about it. But she's going to leave the decision to you."

"Is this why you were sending me back to Boston earlier than planned?"

"Yeah," Philip said. "I knew you'd need a chance to pack and get ready and pull together all the records for the school and do everything else that needs to be done."

"You were planning to come and see me in

two weeks," Morgan said, turning to Cy.

"I still am," he said, still holding her hand. "I was hoping I could help you move."

"You knew what was going on. And Jean knew. Mac and Nick?"

They both nodded.

"Probably everyone in Aruba and Boston and D.C. knew . . . except me." She frowned at Philip. "Why did you wait so long to ask me?"

"Because I had to make sure. I wanted the paperwork in my hands with all the signatures on it. If I'd told you this and then something went wrong, I knew you'd feel betrayed. I didn't want that to happen."

He was right; she would have been hurt. But Morgan didn't think she would have changed her last name from Callahan to something else. Not after this summer.

"This morning, everything finally came in." He leaned forward, planting his elbows on his knees. "But you haven't answered me yet. And as you can tell, I'm a little nervous about this. I still don't know if you would even want to leave Boston. I mean, I've barely been a step above a stranger to you for most of your life. But after this summer, I knew I had to make some changes in my life. I have a daughter that I love and want to know better. I don't want to miss this last year that you'll be living at home. I want to—"

"Yes, Dad." Morgan leaned forward and gave him a hug. She smiled at Cy. "I'd love to move to D.C. with you, but only under one condition."

He pulled back and looked at her. "Anything."

"You have to answer one question."

"Go ahead," he said, bracing himself.

"What's the deal with the barf bags?"

For more summer romance, don't miss . . .

California Holiday

BY KATE CANN

Rowan is thrilled to escape England to be a nanny in America. But when the job goes sour, where can she go now? Where are the cute American boys and great jobs? California, of course!

ISLAND GIRLS (AND BOYS)

BY RACHEL HAWTHORNE

Jennifer's perfect summer plan, spending three months with her two best friends, isn't going so well. One friend brings home her boyfriend . . . and the other brings a dog . . . then a cat . . . then another boy. Then Jen gets the ultimate unplanned surprise—she starts falling in love.

From ISLAND GIRLS (AND BOYS)

BY RACHEL HAWTHORNE

Suddenly I wasn't thinking about souvenirs or camp guests who complained about too much sand, not enough shade, or too many mosquitoes. All I was thinking was that I'd never seen eyes so blue. They were the color of a deep ocean.

And they were smiling. As much as his mouth. But it was a crooked smile. One side a little higher than the other. Surrounded by dark stubble. Sexy stubble that matched the color of the hair falling forward over his brow.

"Hi," he said. His voice was a deep rumble.

I knew CCR policy was to greet each customer with a bright smile and a "Welcome to Coastal Campground Resorts. How can I help you?" But all I could manage was "Hi."

From *California Holiday*

BY KATE CANN

Then out of the blue Sha asks, "I bet you're feeling a little jet-lagged, aren't you?"

This is the first real question she's actually asked about *me*, and I'm almost touched. "Er— it certainly feels like way past my bedtime."

"Well—good. I thought—this being the first night and everything—it would be nice if you went to bed the same time as Flossy. So she knows you're *there*, next door."

Oh, *great*. *Charmed*. "Sure," I mumble. "Why not."

"I have tomorrow off. I thought we'd have like a—*training* day, if that's not too awful a word! Then it's over to you, Rowan. And I know things are going to be just *fine*." She does her horror-clown smile at me and I make myself smile back. Then we troop off to get Flossy in the bath.